The Hairy Hand

❄

'Hairy Hand' is a stonking adventure of a story.
I dare you not to laugh, weep, and will on Sept –
as well as fall in love with the devious and
dastardly Mr and Mrs Plog!
Alex Campbell, author of LAND

MONSTER

HAIRY THE HAND

ROBIN BENNETT

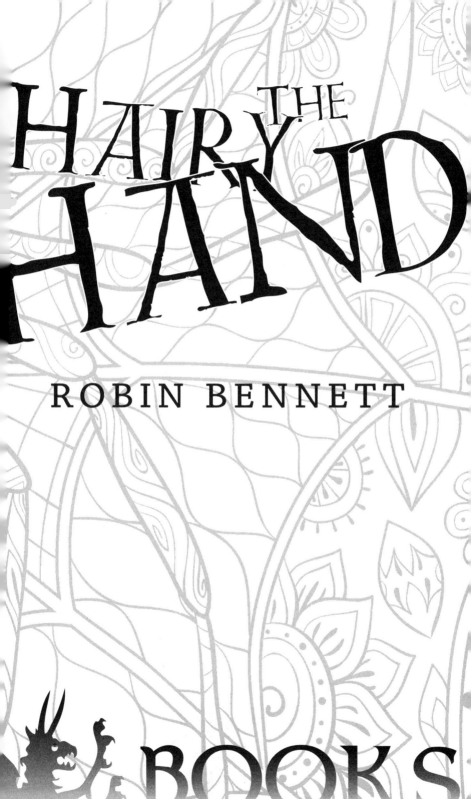

BOOKS

The Hairy Hand (Monster Books Ltd)

Originally published in Great Britain by Monster Books,
The Old Smithy, Henley-on-Thames, OXON. RG9 2AR

ISBN 978-1-9998844-4-4

A catalogue record of this book is available from the British
Library.

Printed by CTPS, Hong Kong.

This book is dedicated to my Landrover Defender 90 (canvas top) whose radio was so awful, I had to make up this story to keep the children amused.

✳

Chapter One

☞ Introducing Sept, the awful Plogs, the Village of Nowhere and the letter that changed everything.

WHEN SEPTIMUS PLOG was small he liked to play in puddles outside his house. Sometimes he would look up and see his mother watching him from the kitchen window. He would stop and wave at her with all his little might ... then wait; but she never waved back. Not once.

He always knew he was very different from everyone else in the village and Septimus often wondered if that was why his mother seemed not to like him very much.

For starters, he had this name. *Septimus* (Sept, for short). Everyone else his age was called Garp, Darg or Dorgk or Blaarg. Good, honest names that sounded like you were sneezing into custard or you had swallowed something pointy.

Secondly, he read books – by the sack, when he could get his hands on them. As far as he knew, noone else in his village read anything except graffiti. And quite how Sept knew how to read was a mystery: there were no schools for a hundred miles, no teachers and, more to the point, Sept couldn't remember ever *not being able to read*. Printed words in books just popped into his head, as if someone was telling the story out loud.

Unfortunately, in the Plog household there were only two books: the one he kept secret from his parents; and the one *they* kept a secret from him. Sept had only ever glimpsed it when he'd come home once and caught his mother staring at the cover as if she dared not open it. It was a small book with a black cover, like dead bats' wings, and no title. Something about the book scared Sept very much indeed. His mother kept the Black Book in her apron pocket.

The other one – his secret book – he had read so many times he knew it almost by heart. It was called *How to be Happy*, and it had twelve chapters, each with a simple idea for looking on the bright side of life. It was Sept's most treasured possession, one that was *just his*. He hid it away in his room under a floorboard – because where he came from, possessions were just things other people hadn't got around to stealing yet.

Apart from him, everyone else in the village seemed to have some sort of point. There was Begre, next door, who made pig food for his dad's pigs. He used rotten turnips, boiled acorns and mud; there was Flargh the Meat grinder (although, generally, if Flargh offered you one of his burgers, you checked where the cat was first, before you knew whether to eat or bury it); there was Stomp the Bully and, of course, Spew the Puker.

'Is puking really a job?' Sept asked his dad as they trudged along through the mud past one or two shops. His father, *Plog the Sneaker*, wiped a runny nose with the back of his hand before slapping Sept around the back of his head.

'Don't talk soft. Course it is. Donkey doo brain!'

A Sneaker was a night thief and it was one of the most respected jobs to have, which tells you pretty much all you need to know about the village and everyone in it. Sept's dad came from a long line of Sneakers. Dark-hair, black eyes and enormous eyebrows – like two very hairy caterpillars had been glued to his forehead. He was also short, stocky and incredibly strong. Ideal Sneaker. Plog pinched goats, chickens, sheep, any food left lying about and even the thatch from roofs. Sept's dad would steal anything not nailed down. And if it was nailed down, he'd come back later with a claw hammer.

They were at the end of the road; beyond was hundreds of miles of nothing and nobody. Their village didn't even have a proper name. People just called it *Nowhere*.

Most of the time Sept tried to look on the bright side, just as his book kept reminding him to do: he was given food once a day, sometimes twice, and it wasn't always turnip – once a month they got a bit of meat off Flargh and sometimes you could actually swallow it, if you chewed for long enough. The main problem with Nowhere was that nothing nice ever happened. People in it just went on being selfish and stupid, day after day, after day ...

He searched out his reflection in a dirty shop window. A small boy, with fair hair and narrow features gazed back unhappily. Who was he and why didn't he fit in?

Sept was out with his father that day because they were off to the market with a bad-tempered goat for sale. Right now, he was concentrating all his efforts on thinking himself warm. Unlike Plog, he didn't have a proper coat or a thick covering of matted hair all over his face and body to keep out the worst of the weather.

The reason they were selling a goat was not so much because it tried to eat everything, more that it was the wrong *sort* of goat: Plog had come back with it the night before from Sneaking. He had been very pleased with himself, thinking they would get lots of delicious milk-based goodies from the stolen ruminant. Sept, who had been reading everything he could about animals since the age of five, knew better. 'It's a Billy goat,' he'd pointed out, happy to be helpful. 'Um ... a boy,' he added, when he saw the mystified look on his parents' faces. 'Look, it's got a pair ...' but he never got any further.

Mistress Plog hadn't taken it well ... not well at all and Mr. Plog now had several new bruises where her huge, meaty hands had battered his already ugly head into several interesting shapes.

'This is all your fault,' muttered Plog, as they walked along, digging his fat hands deeper into his pockets.

'Sorry, Dad,' Sept said for the twentieth time, even though it really wasn't his fault at all. It just seemed that whenever he tried to help his parents, things went horribly wrong.

Deep down it made Sept unhappy to think his parents were angry. Ever since he'd been old enough to think for himself, Sept had decided that he just needed to make his mum happy, then everything would be better – always, from then on.

This miserable, rainy morning would be the day, Sept promised himself, this time he was going to show them he could do something right. Finally. Just like in Chapter One, page 1, line 1 of *How to be Happy*,

"Think positive!"

Sept cleared his throat and tried his best winning smile on his dad, who was concentrating on his boots. He had recently read Chapter 4: it was called *Selling Yourself Happy*, and it had given him plenty of tips on salesmanship. 'I can sell the goat,' he said to his dad, 'and you can go to Flargh's ... where it's warm ... for some of his breakfast beer. I'll come and get you as soon as I'm done. You'll be proud of me, you'll see!'

Plog looked extremely doubtful about this but then the wind rose up to greet them as they rounded the corner of the empty marketplace. It cut through their wet clothes right to their rattling bones. 'Awright,' he said, 'but make sure you get at least 20 shillings, that's a good goat, that is – even if it's ...' he shrugged, 'called Billy or whatever.'

Ten minutes later, Sept was hopping from one foot to the other to stop freezing to death and wondering who, in their right mind, would go to a market on a day like this. So he was quite surprised when a tall man in a brown overcoat wandered out of the shadows at the far end. He sidled over to Sept: a broad hat, jammed almost over his ears, an upturned collar hiding most of his face.

'Ello, ello, young man,' said the man, 'whose goat is this then?'

Ah, thought Sept, *Rule Number One, Chapter 4, "Be Honest - it gains trust for the buyer."*

'No idea,' he said brightly, 'my dad stole it last night.'
The man looked as if he hadn't been expecting that particular answer and his eyes went very wide, making his hat pop up in a funny way. He took out a notebook and licked the tip of his pencil. *Good sign*, thought Sept, *"if they are interested they will often write down what you say."*

'And where is your father now?'

'He's over at Flargh's drinking beer for breakfast.'

The police officer (as it turned out the man in the hat was, of course) hadn't had such a successful morning for so little effort in his whole career. He didn't even mind when the goat ate his shoelaces. He confiscated the animal, fined Plog 10 shillings (all the money he had) and recommended Sept for an Outstanding Citizen Badge, which, in Nowhere, was like walking around with a sign saying *Kill Me Immediately*.

Throughout the long journey home, Plog contented himself with explaining what Mistress Plog would do to Sept when they got back, whilst Sept tried his very best not to listen. After about a mile, he was beginning to hope that Mrs. Plog wasn't half as imaginative as Mr. Plog.

'When she finds out this is all your fault, my lad, she'll stretch your ears until they wrap around your face, she'll frow you down a well and drop baby crocodiles in after you. She'll 'ang you upside down for a week, gnaw your toes off, then she'll give you a Chinese burn. *And* a dead leg. Then most prob'ly she'll make you drink cold sick for breakfast, lunch and tea, sleep in a puddle, learn long division ... ' and so on.

By the time they got back home Sept's teeth were chattering again, but it wasn't from the cold.

Someone was waiting at the gate of their hovel. Sept swallowed some bitter spit that rose up from his stomach and felt shaky: if he turned now and ran, Plog wouldn't be able to catch him – but where would he go? 'There she is ... you *just wait*,' said Plog nastily.

Instead Sept stared, for Gertrude Plog had started to do something she hadn't done for twenty years or more. She was actually running. It was like being charged by a small hippo in a dress. Sept screwed up his eyes and waited for her worst. Except she did something even more amazing – something she had *never* done. She kissed him – well slobbered all over him, actually ... but the good intention was there.

'Oooh my darlin' precious boy, 'as Mr Plogsie been lookin' aftir yir? Oooh, I 'ope so, I was worried 'arf to def, frettin away all morning, waiting for my little prince to come back safely to 'is mummy wummy!' She gave Plog a baleful look. 'I 'ope you didn't let Mummy's Little Soldier get too wet?'

Plog looked like he'd just swallowed a mummified cat as his enormous eyebrows had a disagreement on his forehead: one trying to be surprised, the other frown. 'I, er um ...' then he shut his mouth.

Sept noticed a letter peeking out of his mother's apron.

No one in Nowhere had received a letter for years, unless it was a police summons. Gertrude Plog's sharp eyes noticed him looking at it. Instantly, her expression changed from deep, theatrical love to deep theatrical sorrow and tragedy.

'Oh, my poor boy, I 'as the most terrible news ...'

'What is it?' Sept's hand strayed towards the letter. He could see his name, half visible, at the top of the page. His mother slapped his hand away with the speed of a striking viper.

'Oooh, don't concern yourself with that now, preserve your grief until you get inside and I can get you a hot mug of cocoa!'

❄

Ten minutes later, Sept was sitting in the only chair by a roaring fire sipping hot chocolate he never knew they had.

After a brief whispered conversation with his wife, Mr Plog was also now gazing at Sept with a ghastly grimace on his miserable features, all ideas of punishment and torture forgotten. His face, which wasn't used to smiling, had gone on strike after a few minutes, so only his mouth grinned and the rest of it, including his eyes, just carried on looking as mean and horrible as ever.

'Oooh I's so sorry to be the one to break the sad news,' wailed his mother, several chins wobbling, '... your dear uncle is dedded only last week. You must travel through the Lost Woods and the Thorny Desert all the way to the Ravenous Sea where 'is 'ouse stands on the cliff.'

'Um ... ' said Sept. He sorted through the long list of questions he suddenly found he had and picked the most important. ' ... I've got an uncle?'

'Of course you do!' exclaimed Mistress Plog, as if Sept had said the funniest thing in the world. 'Everyonesies got an Uncle, imagine not having one of them! ... and , ooh, yer uncle ... such a fine man and a *great wizard*. But a real gent, too – a *Gentiman* War-lock, whichesies a wizard wot doesn't wear a hat. And a bootiful house he's got by the sea, all tall 'n elegant, just like him, and it sits above the frothy waves and the wild winds.'

Now Sept didn't like the idea of anyone dying but he couldn't, at that moment, see the point in going all that way. To visit what must now be an empty house. To see someone he'd never heard of until now. Who presumably (he hoped) wouldn't be there anyway. He also didn't like the sound of the Thorny Desert much, nor the Lost Woods, for that matter.

'Sorry, Mum, I don't understand, why do I have to go?' This was the second most important question as far as he was concerned. For the briefest of instances, Gertrude Plog looked furious, but then she seemed to rally and the smile came back as a leer.

'Why, you must pay your respects to your dear, favourite unc, of course my darling boysie, woysie.'

'Oooh yess, *respects*, very important,' nodded Plog like a nodding dog.

'Are you coming too?' asked Sept. The pair of them shot a panicked glance at one another. His mother waved a fat hand.

'No, no, you go. I'd love to come but me bunions and verrucas aren't up to the walk and Mr. Plog 'as got too much on here, what wif Sneaking and building a brand new comfiest bedroom for his favourite son! Anyway, I'm sure the fresh air will do you good ... growing lad like youz doesint wanna be cooped up 'ere all day long.'

Sept looked out the window at the muddy track and pelting rain. Actually, the more he thought about it, the more the idea of getting away appealed to him – he had a feeling he should keep out of his dad's way for a bit anyway, in spite of all the smiling he was trying to do right now. He cleared his throat.

'When do I need to leave?'

His mother laughed airily, then whipped back. 'Yourbagsalreadypackedandbythefrontdoorbutyouca nfinishyourcoco ...

I supposes.'

❄

Chapter 2

☞ The long and dangerous road to Petunia Rise.

IT SEEMED A SHAME to Sept that just when his parents were finally being nice to him, they were shoving him out the door as fast as they could. Still, he thought, they seemed keen for him to pay his respects to this dead uncle, so it must be important.

He had just enough time to race to the bedroom and pull out *How to be Happy* from under the bed, stuffing the tatty book down his shirt as he went outside. He could not bear to leave it behind. Only moments later, Sept was being pushed out of the house with undue haste, whilst his father helped to hitch a suspiciously light rucksack onto his back.

At the end of the garden, Mistress Plog turned her back on him abruptly and reached into her apron.

''ere you gosey,' she said, handing him what looked like a torn half page of the letter she hadn't wanted him to see. 'Read this and make sure you follow the instructions!' In the pocket of her apron, Sept could see the other half of the letter along with the scary Black Book.

She paused as she arranged the smile back on her face. 'Now, remember 'ow good we've been to you over the years, my boy, an' don't forget your uncle was a richiest man – wizard or not – so, um, yes, you just re-members that when you get there!' She then sort of puckered her lips and bent down and it almost looked like Sept was going to get slobbered on again. Luckily Plog intervened.

'Now, youz don't be molly coddlying the boy, ma, 'ees got a long journey ahead ov 'im and no doubt he'll be keen as mustard to sneak abou ... I mean, pay 'is respects.'

So Sept had to make do with a pat on the head and a sort of half-hearted wave as he left Nowhere for the very first time in his whole life and set out into the unknown. The incident with the goat made it clear he wasn't any good at selling stolen goods, perhaps he'd become a famous explorer instead?

As soon as he got around the corner, he took out and read the scrap of paper. Missing the top section, it started rather abruptly with the words:

... so thanks to the bloodie duck, that's why I am dying.

And then continued:

When you enter you may explore the house freely and at your wille, but CARE NEPHEW! This is a wizardde's house and all maye not be as it seemes ...

My lagacie to you, yonge, unregarded relative: From items of value you happene to find in my late dwelling, in the weirding house of mystery named Petunia Rise,

you maye chuse ANY three things but no more! Once
three treasures are chosen by you, you muste leave the
house forthwithe, never to return!

It is my wishe to leave the remainder of my estate to
the Society of Retired Gentil Warlocks and Weary
Witches.

If the letter went on, Sept had no idea, as another jagged edge showed where the bottom half had been ripped off too. He turned the paper over in his hand, but it was quite blank. I wonder what it said, he thought. And I wonder why she didn't let me see it.

Next, Sept had a peek inside his bag. Inside he found one half of a mouldy garlic sausage that had been in the cupboard for ages, two small apples, some matches and a bottle of water.

Oh well, he thought, the journey cannot be as long as it sounds, otherwise I am sure Mum would have packed more food. I guess I'll be there in no time at all, or at least there will be plenty of people along the way to give a boy travelling on his own food and shelter!

But it was a very long walk. Very long indeed. During it, Sept decided exploring wasn't his destiny, after all.

One night a pack of Wargs* picked up his scent. Their wolf cries and yapping woke him, as he scrambled to his feet in a panic. They pursued him for miles, Sept running blindly, going deeper into the Lost Woods than he had ever dared. Soon he lost the path as he ran through brambles, stumbling over roots, the rough bark of the trees grazing his flayed hands in the darkness until his knuckles had no skin left on them. Just when Sept thought his lungs would burst with the effort of running, he fell into a river and was taken downstream for several miles, scrabbling to keep his head above water. He was washed up eventually onto a sandbank, and he lay there until dawn, wet and shivering, not daring to move. The water had covered his scent but he could still hear the starving Wargs criss-crossing the forest, searching for him.

In the Thorny Desert his water ran out and he had to drink from stinking pools of slime and eat bitter leaves found growing on plants by the wayside. By day his skin went red and peeled in the ferocious heat and by night he lay and shivered with nothing but his now empty rucksack for comfort. *How to be Happy, Chapter 7, page 3: "when things seem terrible, cheer yourself up with thoughts of Home Comforts and Happy Memories".*

That really didn't help much so he kept his spirits

---

* Forest wolves: bad tempered with huge appetites.

up by thinking of how he was doing the right thing, paying his respects to an uncle who must have been fond of him to leave him not one but three things of his choice in his will. But, as he lay alone looking at the cold bright stars, Sept did wonder why his uncle had never once visited.

And despite his hope to meet people along the way, he did not see a soul and he had no-one to talk to. The only words he had actually uttered in all that time were, 'Aaargh!' and 'Ouch!' and 'Heeeeeeeeeelpppp meeeeee!'

So Sept's first experience of the world outside of the muddy valley and the village was that it was every bit as pointlessly dangerous and scary as Nowhere. And Sept felt no more at home in it than he did with the Plogs. Each evening, before it got dark, he would take out his book, and look for comfort in *How to be Happy*. He read: *"Every day is a wonderful new beginning!"* and *"Turn your frown upside down and show the world your sunny side!"* or *"Every bad turn is just an opportunity for something good just around the corner"*.

As the days went on, he began to doubt that whoever wrote the book had ever visited the Thorny Desert, the Lost Woods or ever had anything even slightly bad happen to them. But the book was all he had now.

Eventually, after a whole month of unpleasantness, he finally came over a sand dune to be met by an emerald field of shining grass and vermillion poppies that stood as high as a horse.

Sept had made it. He was alive and he still had all his arms and legs. He didn't know this, but even the toughest travellers avoided the route he'd taken: grownups, with packs of mules laden with food and sharp weapons hidden in unexpected places. One boy, with half a sausage, a bottle of water and a book written by a dangerously optimistic lunatic had done the impossible.

The rolling hillside before him swayed to a steady wind that pushed the meadow this way and that, like waves coming into shore, and the air smelled strongly of salt.

Sept had never seen anything so beautiful in his life and he felt his spirits lift at the prospect of finally seeing the wide ocean: its tumbling breakers, with their white crests like icing sugar and frothy pebbles that crackled and rolled as the waves slipped back and forth.

Far off in the distance, he could see a large wooden house with a stone tower.

Looking at it gave him a funny feeling.

Chapter 3

☞ Sept makes a tough choice (or three).

THAT MUST BE PETUNIA RISE, he thought. Strange name for a warlock's house. From the little he knew about naming houses, it sounded like somewhere an old lady lived quietly with a cat or four.

In spite of its name, there was something about the house that almost seemed alive, thought Sept, as he stared at its dark windows, hooded by half-drawn blinds like eyelids. The front door hung open, looking more and more like a gaping mouth with every step. Sept had the feeling that this house had been waiting for him to arrive.

A battered sign above the porch read *Petunia Rise. Please wipe your feet.*

It's just a house, he reassured himself, belonging to a kind old man, who sent me a lett ...

'SEPT YOU NITWIT. SO YOU ARE HERE ... *FINALLY* ... YOU TOOK YOUR TIME?'

Sept's first, second and third thoughts were to run very far away as fast as he could. The voice was quite the loudest thing he'd ever heard, and for anyone who spent any time at all with Mistress Plog that was saying something.

He glanced nervously about the hallway. There was nobody there.

'OF COURSE THERE'S NOBODY HERE. **I'M DEAD.**'

Sept's brain felt like a jumper that had been turned inside out. 'Um, is this magic, then?'

'OH, YOU MUST BE SOME SORT OF GENIUS. I WAS A VERY POWERFUL WARLOCK, YOU KNOW, OR DIDN'T THAT EVIL HARPY GERTRUDE TELL YOU ANYTHING? ... COME TO THINK OF IT, SHE PROBABLY DIDN'T ... ANYWAY, ETERNITY WAITS FOR NO MAN, SO DOWN TO BUSINESS ... STEP FORWARD BOY!'

'Um, yes, of course.' Sept took two tentative steps into the dusty gloom of the house as the door slammed shut behind him. When the voice came through a second time, it was a lot less loud and just a bit more kindly.

'Alas, I am all that remains of your Uncle Xavier, otherwise I would be here in person to greet my heir. There was so much I needed to tell you ...'

'Really?'

'Humph, yes, well,' the voice interrupted before Sept could get any further, '... never mind all that now, you've got a job to do, otherwise that long journey of yours will have been a complete waste of effort. Now, pin your ears back: by the time the sun reaches the horizon, at the end of this day, I will cease to exist – even as the ghost I am now – and the house will finally shut its doors to all non-warlocks, for ever. So, in a nutshell, you got here just in time, my boy. A day later and your legacy would have been beyond even my efforts – the Lore is clear on that. It's also clear that you may take three items only from a deceased member of any warlock's family. BUT, REMEMBER THIS, YOUR CHOICE WILL BE MADE WHEN YOU LAY YOUR FINGER, OR HAND, ON THAT ITEM, AND IT CANNOT BE UNMADE.'

Sept peered around properly for the first time. He'd always supposed that warlocks' houses were filled with treasures and strange objects with discoveries – mostly nasty – when you picked them up. More to the point, if he was beginning to learn anything since he had left home, it was caution.

However, the inside of the house looked as ordinary as the outside. A neat rug in the centre of the hallway supported a round table with a nice vase. On his left, a doorway led through into what looked like the dining room with an elegant, but dull sideboard, and to his right was the kitchen with a blue stove and washing up neatly stacked near the sink.

Nice, comfortable and not, *at all*, wizardy.

'What did you expect – stuffed frogs, black cauldrons and eyeballs in jars?' His uncle's ghost really did seem to have a knack for reading his mind. 'Magic's about using your brain, not French cooking.'

'OK, um … Sir,'

'Well, you've got good manners, at any rate. I don't suppose you've ever been allowed to do anything much on your own, so now's your chance.'

Sept cast about. There was nothing to remotely interest an eleven-year-old boy. ' … what should I choose?'

'That's up to you, obviously.' His uncle's Shade was beginning to sound like it might get tetchy again, so Sept stepped forward and picked up the first object he could lay his hands on.

'Like this?'

'That's the dog's brush.'

'Oh.'

'FIRST CHOICE CHOSEN – and a very poor one, I must say. You've got two more choices, then. Might I suggest that you think about it more carefully next time.'

'Sorry … yes, OK.'

But something had been bothering Sept since he had got inside the house. It was one of the reasons he hadn't run from the first moment the voice came booming out of nowhere. Actually, it was probably the *only* reason.

A large roast ham was sitting on a silver platter on the kitchen counter. It filled Sept's nostrils with delicious meaty thoughts and made his mouth water. The disembodied voice came again.

'Didn't Gertrude give you any food? I thought not, she's too stupid to know they have to keep you safe. Well, you'll need food for the way home, I suppose. Take as much as you like, including the chocolate in the pantry. If you want to make it back alive, you've just made your second selection!'

Oh dear, he only had one choice left. Sept remembered all the riches his mother had mentioned and had the scary feeling his parents weren't going to be pleased. He took a deep breath and thought hard.

Assuming there wasn't much of interest downstairs, there might be something in the stone tower. So, Sept began to climb the stairs, taking great care not to touch anything.

'Better,' said the voice as he reached the top and came to a vaguely mysterious looking door. 'My study. Just don't *break* anything.' Sept pushed the door tentatively and, as it swung open, found himself in a small, round room with a pleasant view of the sea far below.

A large, cluttered desk dominated the circular chamber and in one corner there was a recessed alcove containing shelves stacked with ancient-looking books. And not just any kind of books: books with symbols in silver and gold, writing that moved across the covers, books that whispered to one another.

Magic books!

This was it, his final choice. Finally he had found something he had been expecting to discover. A vague smell of cowhide and dust emanated from that corner of the room but something else, Sept felt his fingers itch. He was sure that in any one of these books lay the answers to many of his problems: a spell to conjure up the most delicious fresh food whenever he wanted, perhaps; or another to stop it raining quite so much; one to magic his parents into a better mood. Or a spell that revealed where he fitted in ... His uncle had gone quiet, as if waiting.

Sept stepped forward, stretching his arm out but, just as he did so, his eye was drawn to a quite ordinary wooden box that was wedged between several of the more tatty volumes on the bottom shelf. Ordinary maybe, but Sept had always been very interested in boxes of any sort.

Boxes contained things. Things that *belonged* went in boxes and, as a boy who had never belonged, this made them fascinating.

There was nothing remotely sinister or magic-looking about the box, in fact it was quite dull. But, in his limited experience, people put extraordinary things inside ordinary packages. Like Gertrude's sinister book, which she kept in that grubby apron pocket. It was a way of hiding them – so perhaps he was turning into a Sneaker just like his dad. He should have been pleased but, in fact, the thought briefly horrified him.

The point was, Sept's hand felt drawn towards the box, as if pulled by an invisible string, and he reached forward. Time slowed as a warm wind sprang up from nowhere in his uncle's study, carrying with it the smell of hot sand, rich spices and whispering voices – like the dry pages of a book having a conversation with itself. Slowly, deliberately, Sept stretched out and placed his finger on the cheap, wooden casket.

There was dead silence for a few moments – Sept held his breath, expecting to hear his uncle shout at him for being an idiot for not taking any of the important and powerful books of spells. However, when his uncle did speak again, there was a new kind of quietness to his voice. If Sept had been a boy to have received any praise or encouragement in his life, he would have recognised it for a tone of respect.

'Hmm, not so stupid after all. Many years ago, this box was washed up on the shore at the foot of the cliff, hundreds of feet below the very window you are standing by. It was the night of a great storm, the most violent I can remember on this coast or any other, for that matter. In spite of the danger, I was drawn down to the crashing waves, howling winds and biting cold ... Something called me from the safety of this house, something more powerful than I have ever felt in my long years as a warlock ... and there, sitting on the shore, was this simple box. I carried it back home. Climbing the old rope ladder that twisted in the wind like an Egyptian snake, I nearly fell to my death several times.

'It took me many years and all my skill to uncover just a few of its secrets.

'I dared not hope this would be your choice. For this box, or rather its contents, is perhaps the best thing you could have chosen, *or perhaps the worst*. Either way, your life from now on will be interesting, mark my words.' The voice paused. When it continued, his uncle sounded grave. 'I regret I cannot tell you more for there is an unbreakable enchantment between you and me that makes it impossible. One day, I hope you will find a way to uncover the truth.'

'What tru— ...'

'HOWEVER,' his Uncle's voice cut across him, 'one word of advice I can tell you, my boy, is do not open what you have chosen until you are home and the door is firmly locked and very securely bolted. For what is contained in this casket will be strange and shocking to you. And until it accepts you as its new master, if it ever does, beware!'

❄

Chapter 4

☞ In which Sept gets caught in a sand storm, survives and cooks a delicious meal.

❄

SEPT TOOK THE BOX CAREFULLY in both hands and stowed it in the bottom of his rucksack. Then he stocked up on the ham, bread and the large slab of chocolate that had been his second choice. Before he left *Petunia Rise*, he picked up the dog brush. He didn't want to seem ungrateful, after all.

By the time Sept had walked through the lush grasslands to the edge of the desert, it was almost night. More worryingly, charcoal-grey clouds filled the darkest edge of the horizon. A gigantic dust storm had gathered in the east and, within minutes of entering the Thorny Desert, it was hurling great, giant-sized fistfuls of sand at Sept who searched in vain for shelter.

The sand blasted his cheeks until they felt as if they were on fire; it filled his ears, his nostrils and the grit got under his eyelids.

As the wind increased in power, the large bushes he had been very careful to avoid the first time he crossed the sands, were pulled out by their shallow roots. Now they flew across the surface of the sand like great balls of barbed-wire. Sept ducked as one hurtled towards him in the gloom – its iron hard thorns as long and sharp as Warg teeth – narrowly missing his head.

His bag was getting heavier. He soon realised that was because it was filling up with sand. Sept swung it off his back – the straps were half undone: how stupid, he thought as he loosened them and tipped the rucksack to get rid of the sand. Just then, a larger gust than before tore across the dunes and Sept could only watch helplessly as *How to be Happy* was whipped away and up, into the air, flying off into the murk like a tattered bird.

'Noooo!' howled Sept after it. He stared into the swirling sands feeling faint: his precious book was lost forever. 'That's so ... unfair!' he shouted uselessly into the wind. For the first time since he was very, very small, Sept began to cry. And it felt quite good to start with – and at least it got some of the sand out of his eyes.

He stayed on his knees as the sand lashed into him. Images of his short, largely unhappy, life ran through his memory like a film as Sept tried to think of a single reason to go back home. Finding none, he searched his memory for a happier time, when he was very little, perhaps? But all Sept remembered from a time before he was about five were confused images of a cart, someone raising their arms and muttering strange words and two shadowed faces that faded when he tried to make out their features.

He was thinking about his lost book, feeling lost himself, when he remembered something, one last piece of advice in *How to be Happy* – yet seemingly added on, in quite a different tone to the rest of the book.

You always have a choice, boy.

Sept frowned, the funny thing was, he couldn't remember which chapter it came in. But, now he thought about it, Sept realised that, for once, the advice seemed to fit: he really did have a choice. He could get up and walk and find shelter or he could choose to stay out in the storm feeling sorry for himself for a while ... and die.

Sept looked at his uncle's mysterious box in the bottom of the rucksack. On the subject of choices, he had chosen the box and whatever it contained. His uncle had said it was important and that it would change his life ... now, surely, that was one big reason to go on?

So slowly, his teeth gritted in determination, he dragged himself to his feet. Head down, he trudged on. And on. And *on*.

Hours went by.

All about him was a world of blinding sand and screaming wind … perhaps he should try and make it back to the grasslands before he collapsed …

DUCK!

The voice was so clear in his head it was like someone had just shouted in his ear. So Sept ducked.

One of the barbed bushes missed the back of his head by millimetres.

Moments passed and Sept stayed very still. Cautiously, he looked up, spitting out a large mouthful of sand and, as he did so, something caught his eye. Sept squinted. There was a darker patch against the howling grey of the storm. Whatever it was, now moved nearer. Sept shivered and the beginnings of a new kind of fear made his thin, bony body stiffen. A form, like a large sleek cat, was slinking into view between the swirling sands – and it was coming towards him.

Sept felt fire in his veins, his fingers itched and burned – now, was that more fear or something else? Seeing something else alive out here, in the desert in this storm seemed so unlikely. Was the cat caught like him, fighting for its life or was it … a horrible thought occurred … was it *hunting* him? The feline shape moved out of sight for a moment, then back again.

Even over the noise of the storm, Sept heard the whispering he'd heard before in his uncle's study.

The creature was very close now. Slit eyes glowed through the murk, staring right at Sept, who felt a sudden jolt of connection, as if his new companion had just spoken. It's trying to get me to follow it, he realised. Sept felt sure that the cat meant him no harm. Trust was a new feeling to him and, in spite of the storm and his fear, it felt good.

With the remaining reserves of his strength, Sept picked himself up. He began to struggle after his new companion who slid through the storm, seeming utterly untroubled by the wind, its fur unruffled, its movement sinuous and fluid.

After a few minutes, the cat form began to go further ahead, until Sept lost sight of it altogether. He stumbled forward, feeling lost again, beginning to panic. Until, suddenly, something else appeared up ahead, through the swirling veil of sand.

It was too much to hope for, but it almost looked like a cave. Bears lived in caves – Sept had read that – but that was because they provided shelter and that's what he needed most right now, wild animals or not.

It hardly seemed possible – it seemed the cat had led him here, to safety, through the storm. But why?

The wind now howled like legions of devils racing towards him. The sand burned his battered skin and he could no longer stay on his feet; so he crawled. Sept knew that if he did not get to the cave soon (if it really

was a cave), he would die. But ... *choices*, he told himself – *choose* to refuse to let that happen.

Two thin boulders, shaped like curved knives, led
to a crack in a small rock face and in that fissure was
a tunnel and a spacious chamber.

Having already crossed the desert and not found
anything like this, Sept had a strong feeling that
coming across any shelter in the howling sand storm
must mean something, but he was too tired to try and
work it out now. He laughed weakly with relief and
felt the fear slide off him into the unknown, along
with regrets for his lost book.

He was alive.

❄

Inside the cave it was warmer, much quieter and *safe*.
Outside, the wind raged and the sands swirled as if
possessed. The contrast with the sunny start of the
day could not have been more apparent.

The storm had made his throat dry as old paper.
Luckily, he had filled his water bottle from a clear
stream on the meadow, so he took a long drink and
immediately felt much better. His tummy rumbled.
He could smell the ham and bread in his full knapsack
and his mouth started to water.

Sept, whose eyes had become adjusted by now to the semi-dark of the cave, took a careful look around. The earth was almost bare, warm and dry with a few stones and small rocks lying at the base of the walls. In one corner, an old creeper had once grown, run out of water and died. What was left was masses of spongy, moss-like leaves – he could make it into a comfy bed – and several thickish vine stems.

These broke easily into a neat pile and, using some of the foliage as tinder, he soon had a fire going with the last match from the box Gertrude had given him. Warmth and light.

Sept stood up and took another look around. There was a cactus growing at the entrance to the cave. He had read in one of Plog's stolen books that they could be eaten. Taking a sharp stone, he went out and cut off a large juicy corner. Then, by the flickering light of the fire, he carefully sliced away the needles and the leathery flesh. The juicy inner flesh tasted of sweet cucumber and something slightly tangy.

Next, he took out the ham. Humming quietly to himself, he placed a large rock in the heart of the fire and waited until it glowed red-hot. He flipped the largest slice of ham onto the rock and watched with satisfaction as it sizzled, giving off salty, hammy smells as the rind turned golden, crispy brown.

When he couldn't stand the wait any longer, he took out the bread and tore off a delicious doughy hunk.

The fat from the ham and the crisp cactus juice mixed with the bread, making the most mouth-watering sandwich Sept had tasted in his whole life.

He rested his back against the smooth rock of the cave, warming his face and toes by the fire and listened to the storm as he chomped through six large squares of his uncle's chocolate.

'Ahhh!' he sighed contentedly.

'Ahhh!' his echo, higher up the walls, agreed right back. He could stay here forever, become a hermit maybe.

The crying of the storm outside and the warm fire really did make things feel cosier. He plumped up his springy leaf mattress until it was just right, and lay down.

It had been a busy day but his mind still raced. He thought about the mysterious gift. Turning his head, he studied the box; wondering what lay inside its smooth, polished surface. Earlier, when he had been wading through the sand storm, he had thought he felt something move inside the box, stowed in the bottom of the bag. Now he stretched out his hand to touch it ... but drew it back sharply. Did something inside the box just make a scratching sound? Sept looked hard at the box. He wasn't so tempted to open it now – something told him it would be best to heed his uncle's words and wait until he was home. Instead, he lay there, simply staring at it for a long time in the flickering firelight, but nothing inside made a noise or moved again.

Just to be on the safe side, Sept picked the box up and placed it at the other end of the cave from his bed.

Soon the noise of the wind began to lull him to sleep.

As the fire died down to embers, Sept eventually closed his eyes, feeling warm, safe and content, for perhaps the first time in his whole life.

Chapter 5

☞ Sept meets an old man wearing what looks like a nappy who tells him his surprising future.

❄

THAT SAME NIGHT, the old man who had once lived in the cave, visited Sept in a dream.

Sept's sleep was disturbed by the smell of rotting leaves and grubby human being. He stirred but did not wake. 'Are you a ghost?'

'S'pose I am. S'pose I'm not. It was my cave, this ... and you're lying down in me toilet.' Sept shifted uncomfortably in his sleep. This was getting to be a habit; the only people he spoke to these days were dead.

'Sorry, I didn't know.'

' 'Sorright, most times I just went outside. Very liberatin' peeing in the fresh air when you know there's no-one about for one hunner and thirty mile or more ... weird though, at first, when you can't find a tree ... and I don't recommend doing it anywhere near those *prickerley* bushes you gets round here.'

Sept really had no answer to this. 'Right.'

The apparition began to solidify, becoming more than just a smell with a voice.

By and by, a skinny old man stood before him wearing a sort of turban of dirty grey cloth wrapped around his head, something similar wrapped around his middle, and not a lot else. Unless you counted his eyebrows. Whilst his beard was thin and as indeterminate in colour as his clothes, the hair growing from

his eyebrows was the purest white: silken and long –
like two miniature avalanches of snow that arched
around his eyes and then fell in a cascade all the way
to his knees.

One of his eyes was green, the other pale golden,
like the sun in winter.

Sept stared. He was sure he was still asleep but the
old man looked very real.

'What?' The wizened old man looked uncomfor-
table. 'Have I got something stuck in me beard?'

'Your eye,' Sept blurted.

'Oh, that!' the old man looked proud. 'Forty-six year
I was out here on me own ... first twenty years the
eyebrows sprouted like wings, next twenty me peeper
went funny.'

'But why?'

'Who knows ... to peer round corners, count the
colours in a shadow, watch people backwards, see inside out ... m'bee to spy on what's the other side of
the Moon. Never found out. It's probably what occurs
when you've got all this magic slopping about inside
of you and it's got nowhere to go.' A longish pause
followed. 'So 'yer thinking about stopping here, in this
cave of mine, boy? Tell us the truth now.'

It was true, before he went to sleep Sept thought
about going back to his life in Nowhere, with its rain
and dirt, his mum and dad shouting at each other all

the time. At him. Then he thought about staying here in the desert with the clean, dry sands, the safe, cosy cave. 'Well ...'

' ... well *don't* ... well nothing, three wells in a row, all dried up ...'

'I just don't feel ... *right* at home ... I don't feel like I belong.' There, he'd finally said it out loud.

The old brown man stared at him through his extraordinary eyebrows for a long time. He spoke very softly now. 'Sounds like you got it bad, my boy. I never fitted in either, till I turned twelve and things started to happen. I could do things, things that people didn't understand, so they got even more unfriendly. You and me's the same, you'll see soon enough. Same reason I went away and never come back. The things I learned out here though, in all the time I sat in this cave and looked out at the sand slowly going up and down – all wavy and slow-sea. What's your name?'

'Sept ...,' said Sept, 'well, Septimus, actually.'

'Oooh, good name that,' the old man looked knowing, 'strong name,' he glared at Sept, ' ... *magic* name.'

'Thanks,' said Sept.

'Right, I've got two bits of advice for you. You'll be needing it, soon enough since you lost that book of yours ...'

'How did you ...?'

'Firstly,' he held up a long brown finger by way of

interruption. 'Locusts taste much better when you cook 'em, not bite the heads off raw. Second ... go home! You 'n' me are more alike than you realise ... both of us gots something, I just never used mine ... hid meself away. Some people are bad, somes good, most's in between good *and* bad, but ... and this comes from an old fool who sat in a cave for near fifty year ... company's better 'n being on your own!'

' ... but sometimes I think there's something else, something I'm missing,' Sept broke in.

The old man gave him a hard stare.

'Then it sounds like there's something they're not tellin' you boy,' he said harshly. 'You'd best find out what it is or you'll never settle, take that from me too.'

With that he turned to go but, before he left Sept's dream, he stared hard at the box. 'M'bee the answer's in that thing,' he muttered.

The next morning, when Sept woke, he was surprised to see the box was now lying right next to him.

Chapter 6

☞ Plog gets a painful bottom. Gertrude is more angry than disappointed.

THE COMING DAYS saw a big difference in Sept. However, for now, only the vultures patrolling the skies high above the desert noticed the change in the scared and sunburned boy they had seen passing in the other direction a few days before.

Sept was walking so fast and so confidently now it was almost a jog. The old man in the cave had convinced him: he had a mission. He'd been to a warlock's house, talked to a ghost and discovered a box with a secret. In short, he was determined to find out the truth about the box. But something else niggled at the back of his mind: his uncle's words: *There is an unbreakable enchantment between you and me that makes it impossible. One day, I hope you will find a way to uncover the truth.*

Enchantment and *truth*. Sept knew nothing about either, but it didn't stop him thinking about them.

After two weeks, he was getting close to home. He wasn't exactly looking forward to seeing Nowhere again, but the thought of sleeping in a real bed did cheer him up, even if the thought right after – of what Gertrude Plog would make of his choices – made him feel a bit queasy.

He was rather busy wondering if calling the box a treasure chest would make her happier, when he heard an angry buzzing sound above his head, in a tree. Looking up, he was surprised to see his father falling out of it.

'It burns!' Plog cried, clutching his very large bottom as he fell, 'I'm dying, oh help!'

Firestorm Wasps lived on the outskirts of the Lonely Wood in nests as large as a small car. Anyone with any sense would take care before climbing the trees but Plog had no time for the countryside, never went to the woods and so he had only heard about these terrible insects in stories. Plus, he didn't have any common sense whatsoever.

Firestorm Wasps were called that because they were bright red and black, which made them look like they had flames running down the length of their long, jagged bodies. Their sting also burned like molten lava being poured into your veins and the swelling would take weeks to go down, leaving a nasty scar – like a brand.

They were also very, very bad tempered. Your average Firestorm Wasp made Mistress Plog look like a gentle lamb with a marvellously sunny disposition by comparison. They were well known to chase people they didn't like for several weeks. Yes, Sept knew all about Firestorm Wasps. He immediately looked for cover, yet he needn't have bothered.

As more wasps stung him, Plog had decided to let go of the branch, presumably to escape the terrible stings. Unfortunately, Plog missed the ground. He let out a small whimper as the knotted branch between his legs flexed and sprung him back, upwards. Directly towards the wasps' nest.

His head rocketed through the bottom of the nest and stuck there, amidst a cloud of very angry, then very surprised wasps, as they watched their prey disappear with their home stuck to his head.

Sept's eyes followed his father's journey as he hurtled through the canopy of leaves towards a patch of nettles on the ground.

'Hello Dad.' Sept said, hurrying over to see if he could help. Seeing the state of his father, he added, 'are you OK?' shaking his head as he hauled Plog to his feet with some difficulty. 'You really must learn to be more careful, this part of the wood is full of all sorts of surprises.'

'Ah, Sept,' Plog eventually managed to groan, 'your mother sent me to keep a look out for you, that's why I climbed the tree. She'll be pleased you're back, as long as you've got something for us … I 'ope for all our sakes. Oh, gawd, you 'aven't got any ice 'ave you ?'

An hour later they were home. Gertrude Plog wouldn't stop talking and everything she said just made Sept more convinced by the minute that she wasn't going to be pleased with his choices. Not one bit. 'Ooh, I's just sure that knapsack is bursting with gold coins and rare antics!

'Once I'm richy and powerfully, no more selling stolen goods – Plog, are yous listenings? – we's going to lend people money and expect everyone to pay uses back at least four times what we giveses them. Or else. And I'll build the hugiest mansion all in yellow, bright green and pink – just at the end of the village and have a big knobbly gate fixed across the road. Then we's charging people money for travelling through. No-one would argue with us cos' we'd get educated and *That Book* could be useful again.' She stopped and looked slyly at Plog. 'I'll turnes their tongues into fat slugs or their heads into turnips!'

She rubbed her fat hands together greedily and her eyes went piggy.

'So, let's sees it all then.'

Sept took a deep breath.

Thirty-eight seconds later the Plog family were gathered around the kitchen table. Gertrude was the only one sitting – partly because there was only one chair and partly because, since his encounter with the Firestorm wasps, Plog wouldn't be able to sit down for a month. Sept's worst fears were being confirmed.

His mother's whole body was wobbling like a big, furious jelly. 'IS ... THIS ... ALL ... YOU ... HAVE BRUNGED ... YOU IMBY SEEL ... YOU NERDY NINCOMPOOP ... !'

'Calm down, my mountain buttercup,' Plog was feeling almost as nervous as Sept. It had been a very bad day, everything hurt and he didn't care about the treasure anymore: he just wanted to lie down in a dark room.

'DON'T YOU TELLS ME TO CALM DOWN ... THE VILE SPLODGE HAS COME BACK WITH NUFFINK BUT A FEW CRUMBS IN HIS KNAP-SACK, A DOG BRUSH AND A MANKY OLD BOX I WOULDN'T PUT A DIRTY 'ANKY IN ... OH, I SHOULDA GAWN MEESELF.'

'Now, you know that's not poss ...' Plog started to say, before he snapped his mouth shut, as if he had a spider crawling about on his chin. 'What's in the box?' he rattled off to change the subject. 'Might be sumfin worth selling?'

Gertrude Plog looked at the box doubtfully. Then a pudgy arm, like a boa constrictor making a grab for a rabbit, shot out and snatched it off the table. Dirty fingers, covered in cheap brass jewellery, pulled this way and that. She went even redder in the face. 'Won't ... open ... ruddy fing's locksied.'

'No, wait !' Sept had never dared tell his mother to do anything before. 'Please don't do that ...' he added.

'Shuts it!' she was too intent on breaking into the box to stop now, 'there's jewelsies inside, I knows it.'

'But ...' Sept wanted to say it was his, except he couldn't quite get the words out. Barely ten minutes being back home, he felt as if nothing had changed.

Plog, expert Sneaker, breaker-into-things and lock picker, took a look. Trying to ignore the terrible stinging pain in his backside and a duller, deeper throb nearby, he turned the box over in his hands. 'No lock 'ere,' he said, squinting at it. 'Hinges look shot ... pass us a knife ... it's probably just glued itself shut with grease and grime. I'll 'av it open in a jiffy, then we'll see if verruca face 'as brought us anyfink worthwhile, or if 'ees spending the next month sleeping in the outside toilet.' Gertrude Plog cracked a gruesome leer for the first time in several minutes. She almost hoped the box was empty.

Within seconds Plog was hopping about, bumping into things and sucking a finger. After jabbing it with various bits of cutlery, a rusty fork had turned in his hands and speared him. 'It attacked me ... oh blimey, I'm bleedin' to def, 'elp me ma, I'm dyin'!' All in all, it had been a very bad day for Plog.

'Don't talk soft, it's just a nick. Big baby ... as for this useless lump of rubbish ...' With that Gertrude Plog scooped up the box that was lying on its side and threw it on the fire.

Sept, finally couldn't stop himself. 'No! It's mine! My uncle gave it to me, you shouldn't have done that! Why do you always have to do horrible things?'

'Har, har, serve you right for bringing us a load of rubbish,' said Plog.

'Thassright – an' tomorrows yur goin' back to the old miser's place and yur gonna fetch back somfin expensives this time ... are you listenin' ?'

But Sept was very far from listening. He was too busy staring intently at the fire. Sept's fingers felt funny and the dry whispering had started again.

Two things caught his attention: first of all, the wooden box did not seem to be catching light – it just lay in the heart of the fire, and the flames seemed to burn *around* it, flickering away from the surface of the wood. Secondly, there was now a very definite scratching noise coming from inside the box, same as in the cave, but louder ... as if something was scrabbling to get out. Even the Plogs heard it now and they stopped talking and stared. The scrabbling grew louder and more urgent and then became a knocking, then a banging. Sept's funny feeling grew stronger and stronger until it felt like his whole body was burning up. *Knock, knock, knock, bang, Bang,* **BANG, BAANNGGG, BOOOOMM!**

The box exploded into several hundred unglueable bits – sending shards, splinters and slivers of wood in all manner of surprising directions. Everyone ducked.

Something shot out of the fireplace and into the air.

Something dark and sinister-looking, whispering voices only Sept could hear, filled the room.

The thing landed on the table. The Plogs stared. It crouched there and seemed to stare back.

There was a pause that seemed to go on for ever ...

'IT'S A HAIRY HAND!' shrieked Gertrude Plog in her loudest, screetchiest voice. 'IT'S A HAIRY HAND!' she repeated, just in case no-one had heard her the first time. Then, for good measure, she pointed at it. 'IT'S A HAIRY HAND! And what's it doin' in my kitchen?'

'I dunno,' said Plog. 'Ask 'im.'

Both adults turned slowly and glared at Sept through small, piggy eyes.

'Why did you brung us this 'orrible 'airy 'and?!'

Sept, deciding to play for time, took a closer look. The creature shuffled to the edge of the table where the boy stood, as if It wanted to get as far away from Gertrude Plog as possible. Sept leant backwards, but he didn't run. He just kept looking, instead. Jet black skin covered the Hand as well as sleek black fur: from the stump of the wrist cupped in silver, to the long, tapered nails. It looked like it had belonged to a small, agile animal – not a human, but somehow it seemed ... intelligent. His mum was spot on about one thing, though – it was a hairy hand all right.

Sept swallowed hard and tried to think happy thoughts. However, it was clear that in spite of his best intentions he was a big disappointment to his parents. Yet again.

Why on earth had his uncle said it was the best thing he could have chosen? To Sept, it looked weird and a bit scary and it moved fast, very possibly in any number of random directions – like a scorpion. At the base of the stump where the silver band ended, was a short chain. The splinters of wood covering the end suggested that the hand had been chained inside the wooden box. This meant it could be dangerous.

But not necessarily.

Sept had learned over the past few weeks not to jump to hasty conclusions – things weren't always obvious. He looked more closely and now he noticed that the Hand was shivering. It seemed to be scared. *If it was scared of him, why should he be scared of It?* Sept wondered. He took a deep breath, and ever so slowly stretched out his right hand. The creature went very still. It could be preparing to pounce, thought Sept, unable to get the jumping scorpion image out of his head. The Plogs seemed to hold their breath, too, Gertrude's small eyes flitting from Sept to the table like someone looking from a safe distance at someone else about to be bitten by something poisonous. In spite of his fear, inch by slow inch, Sept's hand went forward until it was almost touching the creature from the splintered box. The whispering started once more and the smell of hot sand and spices filled the room, though Plog and Gertrude did not seem to notice.

The best thing or the worst, his uncle had said. Well there's only one way to find out, and so Sept extended a finger the last inch and gently stroked the back of the Hand. The whispering stopped and the smell of magic seemed to disappear just like that.

Its skin felt cool and surprisingly soft, like a new leaf.

The Hand stopped shivering and then It did a strange thing. It bent its front fingers and arched its back, almost as if it were taking a miniature bow to the boy.

Instinctively, Sept now let his hand rest palm up upon the table. Next to his own hand It was much smaller. It didn't seem scary at all now. It felt, Sept concentrated on the right word, *familiar*.

The Hairy Hand hesitated at first, then seemed to be about to walk towards Sept' palm when Gertrude intervened.

'YUK!' she said, 'don't touch it – disgusting fing's probably full of diseases and plague. It'll kill us all.'

'No it won't … ' Sept started to say, 'It's just frightened … '

But before he could do anything, Gertrude Plog had grabbed the chain. The Hand, now upside down, scrabbled frantically in the air, his mum holding It aloft like a spider hanging off its own thread. With her free hand she opened the back door, swung the chain once and let go. The Hand, fingers waving in all directions, flew across the garden and landed with a faint thud in their compost heap.

'Good riddance!' she shouted after it, slamming the door. Mistress Plog turned on Sept before he had time to say anything. 'Tomorrow you go back there!' she bawled, 'and you better find us some jewelsies or money or you'll wish you weren't borned!' She turned. 'Plog!'

'Y-yes my spring lamb,' stuttered her husband.

'Lock 'im in the shed for tonight, the slug's got an early start.'

Rough hands grabbed Sept and moments later he was being pushed into the lean-to where their outside toilet sat: grubby and smelly and dark.

'Don't know why she's botherin',' muttered Plog, but not exactly unkindly, 'you'll never be a Sneaker; you'll never be anything I can make use of or figure out. You're useless in this place, but it's not your fault –' Plog seemed to be struggling with something and, for just a moment, Sept thought he could see another outline of someone, just behind his dad. He blinked but the vision was gone in the gloom.

When Plog had stomped back into the house, Sept went to the small window. He looked out at the garden where it had started to rain in long grey streaks.

... find us some jewelsies or money or you'll wish you weren't borned!

I already do, he thought sadly.

Chapter 7

In which the Hand gets the better of a cat and a falcon.

AT THE PRECISE SAME TIME Sept was feeling miserable and lonely, high up in the sky above the Plogs' house a spiralling falcon spied what it took to be a small rat (or possibly a big mouse) sliding through the long grass. *Food!* It thought, *and about time too.* It didn't fancy hanging around in this weather for much longer, but it was hungry and wet feathers were better than an empty stomach.

Wings tucked in, beak arrowed forward, it dived.

But juicy, unsuspecting morsels were hard to find in Nowhere, and next door's tomcat, Spat (who was just as wet and equally hungry), had seen the same thing and was moving into position to pounce.

King Mithras' Paw, to give it the name Uncle Xavier would have known Sept's Hairy Hand by, was old and cunning. Not actually the hand of King Mithras,* but the paw of a strange cat-like animal he had been given by a mysterious travelling warlock.

The cat lived a long life and when it died, King Mithras thought it would be fun to have the *Cool Cat-*

---

* (whose hands were bigger and not in the least hairy or magical, for that matter).

thingy (as he called it) mummified.

Being magical, the mummified cat remains almost instantly sprang to life. King Mithras' head wife – who could put up with most things alive but drew the line at dead, zombie, sort-of-cats in her house – promptly threw it on the fire. Only the paw was saved.

This was a shame because the mummified ex-pet was actually a very, very rare Llarmarra. One is born only once every 1000 years and whilst they can be a bit odd, they are generally thought to be the most magical and, importantly, loyal creatures on the face of the planet.

Uncle Xavier had looked after the Hand because he respected anything magical, but it had never really belonged to him. He recognised its many powers, not least of which was a resistance to fire, which It had acquired thanks to everyone (like Mithras' wife and Gertrude Plog) wanting to burn it on first acquaintance.

And now, something was making the last magical remains of the Llarmarra struggle through the rain, across the muddy courtyard. Towards a lonely boy in a shed. Towards Sept.

Back to the hungry falcon ...

Seconds into its dive, it had reached supersonic; hurtling towards the Earth, like a feathered javelin, its eyes narrowing as they focused on its juicy, prey.

Just at that moment, Spat, yellow eyes also narrowed, extended his claws and pounced.

The Hairy Hand, the last remains of what had once been a court Llarmarra, may have looked blind and unsuspecting to the stupid, but it had been following the cat's progress and the falcon's descent very carefully. And its timing, born of thousands of years' experience, was spot on.

As the falcon stuck its talons out to scoop up the Hand, a huge shadow suddenly seemed to spring out of the ground. Both falcon and cat tried their best to stop in mid-air as the shadow grew until a clawed spider towered over the tops of the gnarled trees at the end of the muddy garden. As the wind rose to a howl, the monstrous spider pounced, its razor fangs extending towards feline and falcon.

Far below, as it drizzled chilly rain and, more recently, clouds of gently falling falcon feathers and cat fur, the Hairy Hand continued its progress.

Because of this boy, the Hand had lost Its home, been thrown on a dung heap and left in the rain. It had every reason to be very annoyed with Sept indeed. And It knew just where he was.

❄

Chapter 8

☞ The Hairy Hand gets where It is going.

❄

INSIDE THE SHED Sept was unaware of what was coming for him.

He was lying miserably on the cold stone floor, listening to the rain. He was exhausted but only able to doze in fits and starts – a combination of being cold, hungry and the noise of the rain keeping him awake. Whenever he did drop off, he immediately had his strange recurring dream of the cart and someone chanting and lots of people crying.

Pata pata pata pata, **tap, tap, tap** ... *Pata pata pata pata* ... **tap, tap, tap.**

Odd, the rain hadn't been making that noise earlier. **Tap, tap, tap.** He looked up without much energy: through the grimy window he could see a small dark shape. It moved again. **Tap, tap, tap.**

Sept got up and dragged himself over to the glass. Through the thick dust and damp cobwebs he could make out the dim form of the Hairy Hand and he stood staring at It. It seemed to be concentrating intently on the boy.

Sept forgot all about feeling sorry for himself and shuddered.

He was about to draw back, away from the window and this strange, almost frightening creature, when Sept noticed that It was shivering again and he felt a pang of pity. And then guilt. None of this was the Hand's fault. It was mainly his. He should have chosen some silver spoons at his uncle's instead, then everyone would have been happy.

Tap, tap, tap.

It really was horrible weather out there.

Sept used his elbow to smash a small pane in the window. He knew his mother would be furious if she found out, but he didn't care anymore – he was already in so much trouble and he doubted he could make matters any worse.

The Hand, which had darted out of the way of the falling glass, now crawled in carefully over the broken glass, Its chain sliding behind. Sitting on the window-sill, It faced Sept and did Its strange little bow again. Then the Hand sort of sat back and seemed to be waiting for something, a gesture that somehow reminded Sept of an obedient dog.

Slowly and very carefully, so as not to alarm It, Sept repeated his action from before and stretched out his own hand, letting it rest on the sill. Always let a scared animal come to you, in its own time, he'd read some-where. If it trusts you, you can trust it.

The Hand seemed to hesitate but then, bit by bit, It crept slowly, yet elegantly, onto Sept's outstretched palm. It sat there, the warmth of the boy's body slowly leeching into Its own until the shivering subsided.

'I'd offer you some food,' Sept said, cradling the Hand as he went to sit back down where he'd been lying moments earlier, 'but I don't have any and I'm not sure how you eat.' He paused. 'In fact I don't think you eat at all?'

The Hand wagged a slender finger in a sort of digit 'no'.

Still somewhat hesitant, Sept touched the fur on Its back. It was silky smooth, like a black panther's.

Sept felt a tingle.

He looked down and saw the Hand seemed to be agitated again. It waved Its fingers about in a circular motion, like antennae, as if It had sensed something somewhere and was trying to pinpoint it. Then, all at once the waving stopped and the Hand pointed. Jab, jab, point.

'What?'

The Hand stabbed Its index finger into the air some-where above Sept's head. He followed the pointing.

'Up there?'

The Hand nodded a finger.

Sept peered at the spot. Hmm, well it did look like someone had made a hole in the wooden frame above the doorway, or perhaps it was just a rotten patch. He went over somewhat dubiously, taking care to place the Hand on the ground first. But the Hand immediately ran up Sept's arm and settled on his shoulder.

Instinctively, Sept tried to brush It off, but It just scuttled across to his other shoulder. 'Gerroff, gaah!' It tickled. The Hand dodged under Sept's grasping fingers and ran under his shirt, down his back. 'Ah, no! *no!* Stop! Aaagh! Ahha ha hah haah!'' In spite of everything: his tiredness, his fear about tomorrow's repeat journey, the continual ache of having parents who – he was beginning to realise – didn't care about him, Sept was soon laughing and wriggling as the Hand scuttled about him. Until, eventually, It came to rest back on his shoulder, hardly any weight at all; yet somehow reassuring. Sept's laughter subsided as the Hand pointed again at the hole.

'OK, OK, I get it, but this had better be something good – like food,' sighed Sept. He really was exhausted and he knew he had to try and get some rest before morning and the long dangerous journey ahead. He put his finger into the hole and wiggled it about. Nothing. No, wait! His finger brushed up against something metallic. He pushed his thumb into the hole as well. Whatever it was, it was long and thin and cold. Using his thumb and forefinger like a pair of tweezers, he pulled.

A key.

The Hand got very excited at this, and started bobbing up and down.

'How did you know it was there ...?' he began, then stopped. The Hand was now pointing at the door.

'OK, a spare key to this door!'

❋

Sept trudged through the driving rain: the garden lit up in flashes of lightning, like a negative. He hoped neither of his parents were looking out of the window, although he was fairly sure they'd be fast asleep by now.

Back inside the house it was warmer, drier and a lot less smelly than the shed. The Hand shook off the drops of rain like a small dog and looked like It was peering about. From their room down the corridor, Sept could hear both Plogs snoring.

A sudden hard tap on the side of Sept's head, and – 'Ow! What?' Sept stage whispered. The Hand on his shoulder crouched and made a *keep the noise down* patting motion, before pointing emphatically at the front door.

Sept started to follow the silent instruction, when something delicious-smelling pricked at his nostrils. In spite of his desire to leave the hovel as quickly as possible, he found himself drawn to the kitchen where the remains of the Plogs' stew sat in a large pot by the stove.

Outside the wind howled and the rain poured down all the harder. Thunder boomed above the dark woods in the distance and out of the window, ragged clouds, like witches' shrouds, flew across the horizon. As Sept moved forward, the Hand slipped off his shoulder and scurried forward. Sept was vaguely aware that his new companion had become increasingly agitated the longer they stayed in the house. Now It scurried over the kitchen counter and tipped a bowl of flour over. It's gone mad, thought Sept as he made a grab for It. The Hand was too quick and It jinked away from Sept and began scribbling a picture of a house in the fallen flour. Sept stopped and looked at the drawing. It was familiar.

'Is that meant to be Petunia Rise?' He looked at the Hand, who bobbed up and down like an obedient puppy. 'No way, I'm not going back there.'

How old are you? The Hand now wrote in elegant writing.

'I'm 11,' said Sept.

Then, go to your UNCLE. Before your next birthday! The Hand scribbled over the house drawing.

'So, what? I don't think there will be a present for me … I'm still not going,' Sept blew the flour and the word and picture disappeared.

The Hand wasn't giving up that easily. It spilled some more flour and wrote. ɢO!

'No.'

YES ⫢W⫤

Sept went to blow on the flour a second time, but the Hand was far faster; It grabbed a handful and threw it in his face.

Sept sneezed. The Hand froze. Both Plogs stopped snoring.

'*Seriously?*' Sept glared at the Hand who scurried up back onto his shoulder. His head felt dizzy and his mouth was dry with fear: if he was caught now, he suspected things would go badly for him. So far, he'd had the occasional clip around the ear or slap on the back of the head from his dad, but Sept had seen some of the things his mum had done to his dad when she was angry and it wasn't pleasant. Seconds ticked by and turned into a full minute at least, before, at last, Plog started snoring again.

Sept looked out at the dark clouds and took a deep breath. OK. He would have some of the warming stew then he'd leave quietly just before dawn. Hopefully the weather would have improved. He wasn't going back across the desert to his Uncle's, there was nothing for him there; he'd go the in the other direction, where there were larger towns and it would be easier to blend in.

Sept was just lifting a large spoonful of meat, carrots and gravy to his lips, with his back to the room, when a flash of lightning lit up the whole valley. The Hand clenched his shoulder painfully and a feeling like cold water running down Sept's spine made him turn, right as another bolt of lightning flashed across the night sky. This time with thunder – for added effect.

Standing there, in a too-short nightie – her spotty face, blotchy legs and hairy knees all lit up for a split second in perfect, horrid clarity – was Gertrude Plog.

'THEEEF!' she cried, 'YOU WRETCHID, IKKLE THEEEEF SNEAKING OUT THE SHED, SLINK-ING UP THE GARDEN, WHEEDLIN' IN MY OWSE, EATIN MY LUVELY STEW. I'LL MAKE YOU INTO STEW NOW MEESELF, I WILL.'

Plog was awake by now and he turned a light on.

'AAAGGHHHH!' Gertrude pointed at Sept's shoulder. 'THE 'AIRY 'AND IS BACK UN ALL! ORRIBLE BLACK PRUNY FING. I'LL PUT THAT IN THE STEWSIES TOO.' She moved forward, but as she did so the Hand crouched and sprung.

It landed on the highest shelf in the kitchen, just as Plog threw his shoe at It. He missed and hit Gertrude on the back of the head.

'HEEEELP! IT'S ATTAKIN MEEE!' she wailed.

The Hand now scrabbled along the shelf. Plog threw his other shoe, smashing a window, just as It jumped again, gracefully landing on the edge of a light fitting in the middle of the room. The light swung like a pendulum, once, twice, three times and the Hand jumped, using the momentum to propel Itself to the top of a large wardrobe that had sat in the corner of their living room since Sept could remember.

Gertrude Plog, showing more life and agility than she had in years, sprang as the Hand jumped and nearly snagged it. Unfortunately, one of her giant big toes caught on a hole in the rug and she fell forward, revealing a truly enormous pair of greyish pink knickers as she went over.

There was an ominous click behind Sept who turned around to see Plog with his ancient shotgun at his shoulder. 'Let's see 'ow it jumps full o' lead.'

'STOOOPPPP!'

And both the Plogs did stop.

Sept had never once shouted at them, ever. They stared at him open mouthed.

'Er, sorry,' said Sept, but now his fingers itched and burned again, and he wanted to ask his parents if they could hear the dry sound of whispering, too. Instead he murmured, 'look at the Hand, It's pointing at something.'

Plog followed Sept's gaze.

'So what if it is!'

'Shoot it!' said Gertrude but her mouth was full of carpet, so it actually came out as 'Shoomfut!'

'I don't think you should do that,' said Sept very quietly and there was something in his voice that made Plog pause. 'Perhaps you should just find out what it is pointing at? Then, if you don't like it, you can shoot us both.'

Ever so slowly, Plog lowered the rusty gun and stepped forward.

Chapter 9

☞ The Hairy Hand shows the Plogs just one of the things It can do and thereby saves Sept's skin. For now, at least.

FIFTEEN MINUTES LATER, Gertrude Plog was crying. *Actually crying.* Like a great big baby, with tears streaming down her cheeks that wobbled like two halves of a giant bottom.

Plog caught Sept's eye. He looked just as bewildered at Sept. No-one had seen Gertrude in tears in decades, if ever, and it was hard to work out why – so far, she had been too upset to utter a single intelligible word that either Sept or Plog could understand. In front of her, on the kitchen table, lay a cheap locket. When Plog had investigated what the Hand was pointing at, he'd pulled this from a hole in the wall behind the wardrobe, covered in crumbled plaster and matted cobwebs.

Gertrude's eyes had immediately gone sort of starey and she grabbed the locket from Plog. When she'd opened it, a lock of golden hair had fallen out and that's when the waterworks had started.

The Hand was back on Sept's shoulder, looking as pleased with itself as any hand, without a body attached, can.

Eventually, Mistress Plog's sobs quietened and she looked about through red eyes. 'Oooh, me lurvely Hairy Hand,' she cooed, stretching out a pudgy arm. The Hand scampered around the back of Sept's shoulder, away from her – not that she seemed to notice. 'What a cleverest, sharpy eyes ikkle mouse, yous iz, finding that what was lost for so long. I nevir thunk I'd be see'in that lockety up agin. Oh so shiny and new it was when me dad gave it me, just like my shiny golden curls I put in it to keep'um safe ... and then my sister, who got green eyes like the cat, stoled it and hidded it, then she ran away and we nevir sawed her again, nor my lovely lockety up.'

'I think it's good at finding things,' said Sept, the key to the outside toilet still in his pocket.

'Oooh, you don't say ... ,' Gertrude's eyes screwed up as she gave the Hand a long look. 'I wonder 'ow It does it? No eyes, no nose, just feelin' about like a cleverdy ickle spidy.'

'Must 'ave found that key to the door for you an' all.' Remarked Plog to Sept. 'When you got outta that shed and inta the house, I said to meeself, ees got the makins of a Sneaker after all that boy. I guess it was the Hand, though wasn't it?'

'Um ...' said Sept who'd had a feeling all along that the Hand was just trying to protect him when it found the locket. Somehow It knew that Gertrude Plog would forget all about being angry if she found it again after all those years lost. 'Yes, it was the Hand,' he eventually admitted. 'Uncle Xavier said it was re-markable when I chose it.' Sept said, leaving out all the stuff about Sept himself. Small, piggy eyes continued their sharp staring at the Hand who had begun to look less sure of Itself and now crouched, rather nervously, as high upon Sept's shoulder as it could go.

'*Remarky* Ball, says you? Hmmm ... well Pa,' she turned to Plog, her features now back to their usual meanness, her voice quiet and dangerous. 'I'z wonderin' what else it can find – ain't you?'

Chapter 10

☞ Skrewskint, hidden treasures and creepy, burned dolls

THE STORM HAD SUBSIDED to the occasional squall as three figures – Gertrude, Plog and Sept – struggled through the mud and debris in the pre-dawn gloom.

Presently, they came to Skrewskint the Miser's plot. A toppling wooden house stood at the end of a narrow front yard strewn with rusting machinery, discarded toys and, for no good reason, several old prams.* The house seemed to swallow up all surrounding light, as if it was as greedy and grasping as its bitter and bent owner.

Skrewskint was known to be the richest inhabitant of Nowhere, partly because his family had once owned all the land around, but mainly because he never spent a penny of his fortune nor threw anything away.

'Gives me the willies, ee does,' said Plog, 'always 'as.'

'We'll go round the back,' said Gertrude shortly.

A few stressful minutes later they were in, but not before they had pushed and pulled Gertrude Plog through a tight gap in the fence. It was like squashing an uncooked sausage through a keyhole and it didn't improve her mood one bit.

---

* The presence of prams in Skrewskint's garden was inexplicable in that no child had ever been seen at the property for generations. People even seriously doubted that Skrewskint himself had ever been a baby.

'Right,' she hissed as loudly as she dared, 'I's wantin' treasure, so you shows me where it's at and these two thickies will get to diggin'.'

Sept, with the Hand still perched on his shoulder, waited for a tingle and listened for a whisper. Nothing. He glanced at the Hand. It sat there unmoving – black and still, like a dead thing. Losing patience, Gertrude made a grab for the chain, but missed as It suddenly came to life and leapt in the air, landing in the branches of a crooked tree.

Gertrude Plog started to jump up and down with rage like a fat Rumpelstiltskin. 'Yous come down 'ere this minute or when I gets me mitts on you I'll squeeze until there's nothing left, I'll snap your pig-gies one by one and throw thems in the fire!' Gertrude Plog was within milliseconds of losing it completely. She drew herself up to her full height (four feet two) and looked like she was about to have an epileptic fit.

Then she stopped.

A cunning look came across her features and she lashed out at Sept.

The side of Sept's face went instantly numb with the force of the slap and his ear rang, as he staggered sideways and fell to the ground. Then a strange thing happened; for a moment Sept found he was looking at himself falling as he was hit – as if he was seeing it through the Hand's eyes. If it had any.

Little flecks of molten lava seemed to swim in the blacks of Gertrude's eyes as her fat fist tightened on Sept's hair until it felt like the top of his head was coming off. Plog stepped forward to say something, caught her look and stepped back quickly.

'Show me,' she rasped at the Hand in Its tree. 'Use that pointy flinger like a nosey and shosey what ees got under all this mud an' tat, or I hurts the ickle boysie.'

The Hand began to bob up and down, in extreme agitation. Just for a second it came again, that sense of being out of his own body ... and Sept got the feeling that It wasn't helping him – because It was waiting for Sept to help himself. But he honestly didn't know how he could stand up to Gertrude.

She grabbed a rusty hammer with only half a handle that was lying in the long grass. 'I'll bonk him on the head wiv this!' The Hand, looking even more anxious than before, seemed to look this way and that, then back down at Sept as if making up Its mind.

'One!' she said raising the stump of hammer.

The Hand raised a finger and made a circular motion.

'Two!' Gertrude Plog arched her back.

The Hand stopped and seemed to hesitate.

'THREE!' The hammer came down. As Sept closed his eyes, waiting for the blinding pain, the Hand finally came to a decision and Sept felt Its disappointment in him – had It been waiting, hoping for him to do something for himself? With the speed of a puma, the Hand spun around, stuck a finger in the direction of what looked like a heap of old blankets and went rigid.

The hammer stopped ... millimetres from Sept's head.

'Plog.'

'Yes, my gentle swan?'

'Go looksee that pile of stinky stuffs over there.'

Slowly, Plog went over and started picking through old items of clothing and bits of plastic. Someone had set fire to it at some stage but it must have started raining because most of it was only half burnt and soggy-looking.

'I hopes you isn't playin for time?' There was real menace in her voice again. Sept had never seen her so scary.

... Plog picked up a half-melted doll's head ... Sept had closed his eyes again, so he didn't see the Hand jumping up and down pointing at what was left of the old doll.

Something rattled. It came from inside the head and it sounded loose, like a stone. Plog's Sneaker senses moved up a gear. ' 'ang abowt ... wossis?'

'Givit 'ere!' Gertrude snatched the head from Plog and tore it in half in one brutal motion. The rip was so violent that something shot out of the cavity in the head and into the air. Something that sparkled. Something red.

Both his parents rushed over to the spot it had landed, next to Sept.

'Coor,' said Plog.

'Well I nivvir!' said Gertrude. 'Crafty old beggar!'

They were staring at the largest ruby any of them had ever clapped eyes on in their lives.

❄

Now, Skrewskint's house had a broken porch at the back and under the rotten floorboards was a dark place.

In this creepy cavity, hidden from sight, there lived a pair of creatures so mean and evil, even the rats and spiders under the house avoided them. They may once have been dogs, but any trace of *dogginess* – wagging tails, chasing sticks, enjoying being patted – had long since disappeared. Spending so long in the dark, thinking wicked thoughts, they were more like a sort of large rodent these days. Short snouts (not a million miles away from Plog's own nose) and a tangle of sharp teeth going in several directions (ditto), led down to short, muscular bodies covered with greasy fur of no particular colour – call it *muddy* oil. Their hind legs were stumpy and very powerful and their tails were completely bald, just like those of a rat, and covered with flaky, scaly skin.

Of course, they smelt awful – a cross between the worst toilet in the world and something already rather smelly that had been dead for a week. In a sewer. But, worse than all of the above, were their foul tempers.

It was for this reason that Skrewskint kept them as guard dogs and occasionally fed them but not too often – for he liked them to be hungry.

So when the Plogs had broken into the garden, the rat-dogs had opened their slit, angry-pink eyes. Then they'd crept from their burrow underneath the house. For now, they watched in silence as Gertrude Plog ranted and raved. They stared at the Hand and sniffed the air – some primeval instinct told them that the strange black creature that climbed the tree was best left alone, but the woman's giant legs looked soft and chewy. Uttering low growls, they rose on their haunches and slunk forward, needle-like teeth bared.

The only one who heard them coming was the Hand. Silently It tapped the side of Sept's head and pointed emphatically at the hole in the hedge. It jumped off his shoulder and scuttled towards this exit, beckoning at Sept to follow.

The boy didn't need asking twice. At the edge of the garden he turned to call his parents who were still celebrating their find.

Too late.

Jumping the last few feet, the lead rat-dog opened its jaws incredibly wide, like its entire head was splitting open, and sank its teeth into Gertrude Plog's huge, doughy backside. The second rat-dog did even better – jumping so high it was able to latch on to the biggest thing in range – Plog's nose.

Plog submitted to his fate with resigned howls of pain and anguish and waited for it to end. Gertrude Plog, however, wriggled and flapped her flabby arms about, which only made the rat-dog bite harder.

'Aaargh! 'Elps me, I'm been eated by giants ratsies! Help! Help! save me Plog!'

'I can't, are you blind or somefing? I'm be'in attacked meeself you daft old halibut!'

'Kills them, pull em off, tear em up, I'm dying!'

Just at that moment the front door of Skrewskint's house creaked open and a tall and craggy figure of a man stepped out. He was carrying a rusty shotgun. He raised it slowly and there was a distinctive click as it was cocked. The rat-dogs stopped snarling and went quiet, their terrible jaws still clamped around Plog's nostrils and Gertrude's behind.

'I wouldn't move a muscle if I were you,' said a squeaky voice that both Plogs recognised at once.

Chapter 11

☞ The Hairy Hand makes a deal.

'WE CAN'T LEAVE THEM THERE.' Sept pulled up sharp in the middle of the muddy street, the Hand perched on his shoulder. The Hand crooked a slender finger in the perfect shape of a question mark. *Why ever not?* It seemed to be saying.

'No-one deserves to be left to those things,' Sept answered. The Hand splayed Its fingers

... really?

'Yes, really. They are my parents,' said Sept firmly and he turned back towards the dark house where there was now an eerie silence and a new, taller figure outlined in the gloom. That must be Skrewskint, he thought.

Sept knew that if he paused even for a moment he would have second thoughts, so he marched up and pushed back through the hole in the fence. 'I'd let them go, if I were you!' he shouted. He did his best to sound confident, but his voice was a bit wobbly as Skrewskint loomed towards him like a ragged crow, his eyes narrowed. The two dogs were spitting and snarling at their master's heels, their own eyes fixed on various tender and cherished parts of the boy, who was beginning to regret his decision to go back, especially as he didn't have a plan.

However, years of living with Gertrude's rages and Plog's bullying, as well as several months avoiding death on his own had taught him one thing: show fear and you've lost. He grabbed the only object to hand – the Hand – and drew a deep breath.

'One more step and I will unleash Its power!' and he pointed the Hairy Hand right between Skrewskint's eyes. The miser paused and both dogs stopped in their tracks; not exactly scared, more curious.

'Wossat, then?' His voice was an old lady's – high and reedy, like a squeaky door that has not been opened for years. The Hand seemed to have realised what was expected of It and Its long fingers twirled and writhed as if preparing a spell.

'Oh, this is an evil appendage, a wicked servant with black thoughts and a terrible imagination ...'

'Do you mean terrible in the sense that it thinks up bad stuff or that it doesn't have a very good imagination?'

'Um, the first one,'

'Oh, alright,' Skrewskint didn't look convinced at all. 'So what's it do then?'

Sept took a deep breath. 'If I let It have Its way my Hand will turn your tongue to stone, your eyes will go backwards in your head, centipedes will crawl from your mouth and slugs ooze from your ears.' The Hand went stiff, pointing directly at Skrewskint. One of the dogs whined. Sept began to warm to his theme.

'If I give the word It will cover your face in farting warts.' He was actually enjoying himself now as the shotgun hung more limply in Skrewskint's large hands and the two dogs backed behind their master's legs. 'You'll never be able to wash out the stink and people will smell you coming a mile away and cross the road holding their noses.' Behind Skrewskint, the Plogs had finally worked out what was going on and they began to edge their way towards the gap in the fence.

'Well, there's no need for that,' Skrewskint was looking even paler than usual. 'But those Plogs, they owe me what's mine.' The shotgun began to rise again, pointing right at Sept who felt panic creeping back.

'Not one inch higher!' he shouted in his most commanding voice, pointing the Hand right at Skrewskint. But he never found out if the bluff would have worked.

'Quick, Ma, scarper!' shouted Plog, pushing Gertrude through the hole and squeezing behind her like a fat rabbit. Clearly they didn't mind leaving Sept on his own with Skrewskint and his rat-dogs. The shotgun went up and there was a loud explosion just as Sept shoulder-barged the creepy old man, forcing the shot high, so it missed Plog by about three feet. Both man and boy fell in an untidy heap on the ground. Sept, his ears ringing, was up first and running for the gate at the other end of the garden, the Hand clinging grimly to his collar. He'd jumped up fast, but not fast enough.

'Stop, you young thief!'

Sept abruptly halted just as another loud bang cut through the dawn silence, followed by a strange rush of zipping noises.

As he turned, everything went super clear – it was as if his eyes could take in every detail of the scene: Sept saw the orange blast of the rusty shotgun; the puff of black smoke. He could literally feel the pellets zipping through the air, like a swarm of Firestorm Wasps racing towards him, their dry wings making the noise of a muttering crowd.

You can do it, another voice rose over the sighing swarm. He should have been terrified but he felt strangely calm, only his fingers felt funny. Sept kept the thought of wasps in his head and, as the lead pellets raced towards his chest, he simply brushed them away, like shoo-ing a cloud of flies and felt the blast change course and miss him. Then, just as rapidly as things had got weird and slow, everything sort of sprang back to normal.

Sept had no idea what had just happened, and he didn't get a chance to think about it. The Hand was pointing frantically at the hedge.

'Good idea!' said Sept, 'I think it's time to go before he reloads.' The Hand gave him the thumbs up sign.

'If I see any of you again, I'll feed you to my dogs, one tiny morsel at a time!' Skrewskint looked a bit mystified as to how he could have missed such an easy target, but Sept was now too far away for him to load and fire again. Sept landed the other side of the gate, rolled and scrambled to his feet. Then he grabbed the Hand, shoving it into his coat pocket and ran down the road, arms pumping, chest heaving.

Sept didn't go home immediately. He hadn't forgotten all Gertrude's threats about going back to his uncle's. However, he had just saved his parents' lives, so after some thought sitting by the road, the Hand still on his shoulder, he got up to see how they were.

When he opened the front door, he found the Plogs sitting by an empty fire.

If Sept expected any thanks, he was about to be disappointed.

'It's alls your fault!' Gertrude yelled as Sept stood by the door. 'That magicky hand could have exploded those dogsies with a spell. You just wait 'til I gets *my* hands on you ...' but she stopped. The Hand had jumped from Sept's shoulder, who stood in front of the window. A red sun was rising and it threw the Hand's shadow out across the room, like a giant spider bathed in a bloody red glow. The whole room suddenly went very hot and the whispering came once more, like grains of sand being blown over dry parchments.

'Er,' um,' Plog had gone sweaty and Gertrude's jaw wobbled in fear. 'Let's not be hasty, my cherry blossom ... we don't know what that thing can do.' He glanced at Sept. 'Boy ... um, I mean Septimus, my dear boy, tell It Ma was only joking ...'

Sept smelled the air, magic had a sort of burning odour to it he was beginning to realise. 'It's OK,' he said to his parents. 'As long as you don't make any sudden moves,' he added, not forgetting the speed of the slap he got from Gertrude in Skrewskint's garden.

He turned back to the window as the Hand signalled to Sept for a pen and paper by making writing signs. When Sept shrugged, as if to say that he seriously doubted they had such things in their house, the Hand seemed to look briefly exasperated, before It scampered over to the fire and started to write in the ash strewn around the grate.

Sept looked on, his eyes getting wider with each line, as he read the words out loud for the benefit of his parents.

Dear Plogs

When Xavier told me you were stupid, he left out the part about you being brutal, selfish and lazy. I also thought he must have been exaggerating about just how stupid you are. After less than a day in your uninspiring company, I can see he wasn't. If anything, he was being kind. That Sept is still essentially good and, frankly, alive, is a minor miracle and the only reason I am writing what comes next. So, try and concentrate. And, for the love of the Ramses, stop picking your nose.

(Plog pulled his finger out of a large, hairy nostril and wiped it on his trousers, muttering to himself).

I will find gold and jewels for you.

But only if YOU do not harm Sept or treat him in any way other than your loving and loved son.

This is my first solemn promise to you both.

We will find gold and jewels that people, long-dead, have buried or perhaps lost. We will unearth precious gems in forgotten places, fabulous artefacts and coins of great value.

In short, I will make you, Master and Mistress Plog, rich beyond your wildest dreams.

However,

I will not steal from or hurt anyone for your greed.

AND, if you do hurt Sept, I will have my revenge. And it will be terrible.

Sept is more special than you could possibly guess.

This is my second solemn promise.

Finally, you have something in your possession that does not belong to you. The Book. I am unable to reveal the harm you have already done with it, but my third and final promise is, if you ever try to use it again for your evil purposes, it will be the end of you.

Llarmarra 'Hand'

It took a few moments for what Sept had just read out to sink in, before Plog began to grin and Gertrude began to laugh. And laugh, louder and harder with each passing second, until her flesh wobbled and tears ran down her face. 'Didn't I tellies you it would all be worth it,' was all she could bring herself to say.

And all the time, Sept stood quietly in the corner. He wasn't thinking about the money, or the threats the Hand had made. He wasn't thinking about the Hand, really. *What book?* was what he thought. Although he had a pretty good idea, and just thinking of it felt like cold water trickling down his spine.

Chapter 12

☞ It's unbelievable - the things people will throw away or just leave lying about the place.

'DRAGONS' TEETH!' Sept was sure he knew this hand sign. 'That one means a storm is coming. A big one.' The Hand flicked a long finger up for *yes*, a thumb for *well done* and then crooked its little finger in a circle.

'Um ... old man? No wait, that's the middle finger ... don't tell me, I know, I know this one ... um ... snail ... no, like a snail ... TORTOISE. It means *be still* ... or *don't move.*'

Sept was a fast learner.

Six weeks passed very quickly from that rainy dawn when the Plogs had been promised riches beyond their wildest dreams in exchange for being good to Sept. However, it's worth pointing out that for all of them, this was not saying much: up until now Sept's wildest dream had been not having to smash the ice in his bath most mornings; Gertrude's had been not having to eat the pretend chocolate in dog biscuits; and Plog's to go to bed, just once, without being in terrible pain.

All their lives had improved - for one thing, they found out very quickly what a huge amount of treasure people just leave lying about the place. Even in a place like Nowhere.

For example, at the first crossroads out of the village, high on a windswept hill, the Hand pointed, with one thin, hairy finger, at where a diamond engagement ring lay wedged deep within the long grass and brambles.

Afterwards, when they were at home and both the Plogs were snoring in the larger room next door, the Hand started to write the ring's story in the ash beside the fireplace:

It once belonged to a beautiful young girl with rich parents. The girl was young and perhaps a bit foolish, but she had read enough romances to know she should marry for love, and knew enough of her own mind to refuse to accept a wealthy but disgusting old man who had dirty grey hairs growing out of his nose and ears. Honestly, if you could see what I can see, he makes Plog look like a ballerina. Urgh!

'What happened next?' Sept loved these stories as much as any book.

Well, late one night, in thick fog, she tore the ring from her finger and hurled it away. She was running away from home, from her parents and the old man's servants who were chasing her, with the sole purpose of bringing her back to marry their master.

'And then,' Sept wanted to know more.

Sorry, no idea, but it probably doesn't end well; take it from me, this sort of story rarely does.

It seemed the Hand could tell the story behind the ring just by touching it. However, as soon as the ring had left her finger, the memory had vanished, so the Hand was unable to tell what had become of her.

The Plogs left Sept alone with the Hand each evening, usually with no fire, whilst they stuffed their faces in the comfort of their bed and pawed at whatever new treasure the Hand had found for them.

This might not sound ideal, but Sept was finally knowing what it was like to have someone to talk to who was interesting and interested in something other than making other people unhappy. Better still, the Hand could not waste time every evening writing everything down, so it set to work teaching Sept the Secret Sign Language of the Magician Pharaohs.

His apprenticeship started the very evening the Plogs lit a fire but went to bed before it had died down.

Immediately the Hand started pointing at the hearth, doing Its strange, bobbing up and down routine that Sept was beginning to realise meant it wanted his attention. At first he thought the Hand had seen more treasure, so he placed It gently on the stone floor.

Then the Hand scurried over to the fireplace and Sept leaned in, expecting It to write in the ash again. However, his friend, or his protector? – Sept wasn't quite sure what the Hand was, yet – stood very close to the flames, silhouetted and pointing behind the boy. Sept looked around, to see if one of the Plogs had come back. Instead he saw that the fire's licking orange flames had thrown the Hand's shadow out across the whitewashed wall behind them. Sept turned back to the Hand to see It curl Its fingers and hunch down. Sept jumped forward in alarm, thinking the heat of the flames might be hurting the Hand.

But, at that moment, a thought occurred to him.

Sept turned around slowly and, sure enough, the shadow against the back wall that the Hand had made was clearly a human figure. Bunny ears was one thing, everyone can make those, but just how the Hand had managed to make a shadow that looked so real made Sept gasp. The shadow figure was sitting down and it had long hair. Sept had tried making shadow pictures before on his own in the candlelight and had given up at a rock. Now the shadow changed and he was looking at a ring and so, this was how, bit by bit, the story of the girl and the lost ring was replayed like a puppet show.

As the weeks went on, Sept quickly learned that not all signs were whole words. Sometimes the Hand would need to spell out a word. It taught him the signs for the letters by drawing a picture and writing in dust or ash the corresponding letter in modern writing, so that the letter A looked like a big bird with a bald head (a vulture, Sept supposed), 'J' was a snake, 'D' a hand and so on. Sept, who had taught himself to read, learned so quickly the Hand became excited.

I knew it! The Hand exclaimed one day, after It had told a long story of a farmer who had sold his 7 daughters to a witch for 7 rubies – stones which they found in a dry well by a deserted cottage at the edge of the Lost Woods. Sept had understood the whole story first time, without the Hand having to go back and explain any of Its signs.

Knew what? Sept had long given up speaking out loud to the Hand, but used the secret language to ask – it seemed more natural.

The Hand seemed to hesitate, scampering left and right in short, quick movements, as if trying to get around something.

Now just listen and don't get angry, I need to tell you something. It's pretty important. The Hand signed, so rapidly, Sept struggled for a moment to follow the actions.

Sept bent his index finger, shorthand for *What?*

I can't tell you.

What on earth are you talking about? Sept was confused, *let's get this straight, you've got something really important to tell me, but you're not going to?*

Um ... signed the Hand, *yes.*

So why are we bothering to have this conversation?

Because it's important ... you're important ... there are things you need to do ... there are things you can do.

LIKE WHAT? Sept had learned to sign in capitals and it was proving useful.

You need to leave, the Hand signed again.

'Where would I go?' asked Sept, thinking about the village Nowhere, the rain and the mud and the misery.

I don't know! Anywhere away from the Plogs is a good start. First of all, they'll never change, they'll just keep on being horrible until they do something really bad to you.

No they won't, replied Sept, not really believing it, *they're my parents. I need to stay ... it's my duty. I can make them better.*

No you can't, said the Hand.

What's the second bit anyway?

You need to go before you turn twelve. Not many people have a destiny, Sept, but you do. You need to leave to become you. The Hand looked like it was watching Sept very carefully when It said this.

Oh, not that again. Sept remembered the incident with the flour. *What's it about me turning 12 that's so important?'* Sept asked. Sept had also not forgotten the cave and what the old man had said about finding out the truth about himself. *Is there truly something about me, or you just don't like my mum?*

But, in answer, the Hand just bunched up, trembling, as if straining against an invisible force. Sept could see it was upset, so he dropped the subject. In any case, he didn't like to be reminded of the time before and of the lonely, frightened boy he had once been.

Chapter 13

☞ The Plogs get even more dreadful, if that's possible, and they meet some Wargs.

UNFORTUNATELY, SEPT'S ATTEMPTS to improve his parents did not seem to be working. And if he hoped they would be sensible with their new money, he was about to be disappointed.

The Plogs became even louder and started bullying everyone around them. When Gertrude did not get her way, she would pull the horrible Black Book out of her dirty apron pocket and wave it about, promising to use all the terrible spells she knew on people who annoyed her. And, although Sept was sure she didn't know any spells herself, the book scared the hell out of him and he could tell it scared the Hand, too.

They also started dressing in what they thought were the best clothes and jewels lots of money could buy. Plog found an old military uniform that had been left in a second-hand clothes shop and bought it on the spot. It was bright purple, with gold frogging down the front and huge brass buttons – like doorknobs – he polished so that they gleamed and caught the sun in a way that frightened horses.

At about this time, they started to called themselves the Count Ludwig and Countess Ludwiga von Wafffleater and they put on accents when they went anywhere new to sell what the Hand found. Gertrude

Plog decided that if people thought they were very important people from a faraway land they would treat them with the great respect she thought they deserved and they would also get a better price for the goods.

They were annoyed when Sept refused to play along.

But Sept had other things on his mind.

'Gurt avening toe yew, mere servant.' Gertrude Plog held a hand out covered in gaudy jewellery.

'You what?' said the young man in the hotel reception.

'Ma waif, say'ed gerd efening, grersey poor person.' Plog was very helpful these days. At this point he tried out a bow he had been practising recently in the bedroom mirror. It was meant to be regal and add to his air of military grandeur, but he really went for it this evening and banged his head on the reception desk by mistake. The pointy button of the bell connected very painfully with his forehead and went off, making everyone look up from what they were doing. The receptionist was still non-plussed. Sept tried to pretend he wasn't there.

'Come again?'

'Vee require your vinest rooooom fur mein uzbund und aye und somefink smoll und not too hexpensif fur dis boy, wot is our son and hair!' Gertrude Plog carried on gamely. The receptionist now looked like he was trying to do complicated sums in his head whilst wanting to pee very badly indeed.

'Sorry sir and madam,' he said eventually, 'I still can't get the 'ang of what you are saying ... something about your son's hair being too expensive, perhaps?'

Plog glanced nervously around the reception area. It was the most expensive hotel in town and all the people who frequented it were posh. Posh people still made Plog nervous. He sidled up as close as he could go to the receptionist who leaned forward helpfully.

'One decent room, mate, wiv a bath and one of your budget ones for the boy. Ta.' The receptionist looked demystified but grumpy as Gertrude Plog sailed up the stairs with her head in the air.

'Why didn't you say in the first place?' Sept followed behind, reluctantly.

On days they went into the village market to show off, Sept would see everybody staring at them with a mixture of hilarity and jealousy: Spew laughing but carefully, behind Gertrude's back; Skrewskint's thin, cold face watching keenly from an upstairs window. Money didn't buy friends in Nowhere, but it did get you the sort of hard looks that said, *I'll be nice to you until I've worked out a way of stealing what you've got. Then you'll wish you never had so much as a copper penny.*

Sept especially didn't like the way Flargh looked at them these days as he sharpened his meat grinder.

See? They're too stupid to look after you, signalled the Hand as they followed them down the street. *One day this lot will try and take what the Plogs have got, by hurting them, if they have to – and you.* It pointed at Blegre who was pretending to be delighted to see Plog in all his new finery - though not quite sure how to act: right now he looked like he was trying to shake Plog's hand, kiss it and curtsey all at once.

One day the Hand showed them where to find a broken pearl necklace that had dropped into a muddy bog, many years before, on a picnic trip (when Nowhere and the surrounding area was once worth picnicking in).

Gertrude Plog had been unimpressed with the pearls, which were rather lumpy and small and grumbled that they would only sell for a few silver coins.

As she walked down the forest track in the gathering gloom, moaning loudly about how unfair life was and how they had been swindled, she paid little attention to the broken-down barn they passed by. 'What's the world a coming to ... I's been robbed,' she moaned, conveniently forgetting that up until recently, robbing from other people had been their main line of business. She stared at the pearls in her huge hands as if they were rabbit droppings. 'A few measly thruppeny bits for that necklace is all I expects ...' she glowered at the Hand. But the Hand, perched on Sept's shoulder, was ignoring her as usual. The track they were on became narrower, hardly more than a footpath that led deeper into the Lost Woods: the foreboding sort of trees with plenty of dark places and eyes that watched.

Just then, the Hand went rigid and made a bunched-up sign with two hollow eye sockets. Sept already knew this one: The secret sign for the Death's Head. *Danger*.

'Mum ... Dad,' said Sept.

' ... it's all that Thingies fault, should be findings us better trinkets what's worth more ... why's It acting all funny?' Mistress Plog bunched up her face and glared at the Hand.

A low growl, the sort that can only come from something very large with far too many teeth, came from under the trees.

'The Hand's saying we're in danger,' said Sept.

'You don't say,' said Plog.

'W – A – R – G – S,' signalled the Hand rapidly.

'Wargs!' translated Sept, looking at his parents. 'I really think we should go back the way we came,' he suggested. The low rumble was joined by several more barely twenty yards away.

'Too late for that,' said Plog. That was the moment Plog's Plog the Sneaker brain kicked in at the expense of his Plog the Protector of Sept brain.

Sneaker Brain said *save yourself at all costs – forget everyone else, including your son.* He smiled encouragingly at Sept, 'now you want to be going on ahead, *towards* them sounds, making lots of noise, jumpin' up and down ...'

'Er, why on earth would I want to do a thing like that?' asked Sept.

' 'Cos they won't be expecting it,' Plog looked pained, as if Sept had just asked an especially stupid question. ' 'ere,' he thrust a half-eaten sandwich he'd been saving for later into Sept's trembling hands, 'they love a bit of this meat, they do, they'll be after you like a pack of ... well, Wargs ... as it 'appens. Fit lad like you, you'll soon outrun them – just a bit of exercise. Some excitement, you don't always want to be with your boring old mum and dad!' He smiled broadly and pushed Sept forward.

'I think I do.'

'But make sure you run good an' far ...,' he nodded, ignoring Sept, a sickly grin on his face, 'you'd do that for your old mum and dad ... although pr'haps you'd like to leave ... that thing,' he pointed at the Hand with a look of faint disgust, 'with us ... don't want to be carrying too much weight with you, slow you down.' At this the Hand made to run into Sept's inside jacket pocket but Gertrude Plog was too quick. Somehow, whilst Plog was talking, she'd got behind Sept, her arm shot out and she grabbed the Hand, which squirmed in her pudgy grasp.

'There,' she said, 'safe and sounds ... now off you go and do the diversions, we'll waits here for you with our new friend.' She leered at the Hand. It was desperately trying to signal something to Sept but unable thanks to Gertrude's fat fingers squeezing It.

'But what if they catch me?' Sept wasn't sure and he felt funny leaving the Hand with them. His dad rolled his eyes.

'Well, 'ow should I know what you should do? Moan, moan, moan, that's all you 'ear from the yoof of today. No initiative. Go awn, get down there and make 'em chase you! You never know, it'll probably be fun.'

Without the Hand he felt he had no choice. So Sept walked slowly towards the trees, disappearing from sight around a corner until he came around a fork in the track and an old barn.

Sept also paid little attention to the old farm building, but stared, instead, at what was on the other side of the path. There were about six Wargs, standing there – huge beasts, twice the size of an ordinary wolf and skeletal thin, their greasy pelts showing a row of huge ribs, as if they hadn't eaten for days and now their luck had just changed as supper, in the form of a skinny boy, walked round the corner carrying the rest of a sandwich as a nice starter.

'GRRRR!' said the biggest Warg at Sept who replied, 'Ah, nice doggy!' and immediately turned and ran down the other fork in the path.

'WOA, WOAH, WOAHHH! The rest of the beasts set off in loping pursuit.

'AAARGH!' said Sept, waving his arms about like he was trying to take off. 'Bad doggie, actually …. AAAAAAAAARGH!' Before it occurred to him that running needed all the breath he had got, so he shut up.

In spite of him running faster than he had ever run in his life, the pack was soon closing in. Slowly. Steadily. And Sept felt hot breath down his neck – it smelled of rotten meat, rancid cheese and wicked thoughts. Long teeth at the end of a long snout went *snap* millimetres behind his ear. The next bite would be his whole head.

But Sept had survived the desert and countless other dangers, he wasn't going to give up that easily.

Putting all his effort into it, Sept leapt, stretched out a hand and by some miracle or hidden force –

perhaps the very same that put him in the path of the cave in the desert – his fingers caught hold of a branch.

The thin bough bent under his weight.

It flexed down just as the Warg's teeth caught the seat of his pants. The Warg pulled. Sept hung on. The Warg growled through a mouthful of pants and extraordinarily huge teeth and pulled harder.

Gradually, the branch bent back, towards earth and the waiting pack.

❄

Meanwhile, the Plogs (plus the Hand, still wriggling frantically) had watched Sept disappear around the corner, heard the howling pack in hot pursuit and breathed a sigh of relief.

'Sounds like we're safe,' said Plog, looking tremendously relieved.

'And we've got what's important,' said Gertrude, patting the Hand roughly like it was a large mouse. 'Our bestest friend,' Very slowly, the Hand stuck two fingers up at her. Gertrude Plog who would probably never master the Secret Language of the Magician Pharaohs, even if she had a thousand years to do so, knew what that meant. She grabbed the Hand roughly, squeezing It with surprising force.

'Oh, you are our bestest friend pointing out lovely things to sell,' she said, with a horrible grin, 'you just learns that, or you'lls be squished dead.'

Then the Hand did a strange thing, It stopped wriggling and actually bowed to Gertrude, as It had done to Sept.

'There,' said Gertrude with a triumphant smile, 'I knew you learns quick, now which way to get out of here?'

The Hand pointed down the path where Sept had gone.

'We're not stupid,' said Plog, the man who couldn't even write his own name, 'that's where they went.' The Hand waved a finger for *no* and pointed again down the path.

'What?' said Plog, interested, what's down there?' He walked gingerly round the corner and saw the deserted barn. 'What in there?' he asked, turning back.

The Hand rubbed two fingers together, the universal sign for money and Plog began to smile.

'Well, this just gets better an' better. Mistress Plog, I do think we'll be getting more out of today than just manky pearls.'

When he was sure the barn was empty, Plog slipped inside, signalling for Gertrude and the Hand to follow.

Warm air greeted him along with the unmistakable smell of cows and feathers. 'Well, well,' he said to his wife, 'could probably nick a couple of cows, a chicken and a goose or two. A cow would fetch a gold piece to the right buyer at least. We can also stay in here, nice an' safe till the coast is clear.'

Gertrude nodded and sat down on a pile of straw. 'I needs a rest after all that excitings,' she yawned and closed her eyes, not noticing the Hand, which had scampered up one of the high rafters in the barn.

※

Now, whilst the Plogs were abusing the Hand and wondering where to hide, Sept was still having his underpants stretched by a large, hungry Warg. Sept, displaying a strength in his fingers he never knew he had, hung on for dear, sweet life. Meanwhile, the Warg, who was also quite surprised at Sept's tenacity, but mainly pretty hungry, pulled and growled whilst his co-Wargs slunk about in semi-circles and panted at the very thought of hot young meat to chew on in the very near future.

And the branch was very bendy indeed.

Sept, who could see what was happening by turning his head, took a quick peek, then closed his eyes tight.

But, just as his backside reached a height where the other Wargs could make a grab for him, he heard something snap. At first he thought it was the branch but instead of feeling the hot breath of hungry animals, he felt cool wind rushing past his ears and an even cooler wind further down below.

Very carefully he opened one eye, then both, in surprise and fear. The branch had held, but his underwear had snapped. Bent down as far as it would go, when released, he had been shot upwards again, with even more force this time. So right now he was sailing through the air with no bottoms on.

Far, far below him he could see several surprised Wargs looking up at him, one of whom was wearing the remains of Sept's underpants on his head.

Over the tops of the trees the boy sailed, deep into the woods, until, as he reached the full height of his trajectory, he suddenly lost the almost pleasant sensation of flying and got a whole new (unpleasant) sensation of falling. Down he shot, narrowly missing some sharp branches, just clearing a pile of jagged rocks, straight into a mud-filled bog.

And this was not the sort of bog that appears after a bit of a storm. No, this was the sort of mud that would still be there even if the sun shone for the whole summer and not a drop of rain fell. It was the sort of mud that you could lose an entire house in, plus a couple of lorries. Bottomless, burping, mushy mud. It was the sort of mud you could count on to be sticky and very smelly.

However, it was soft, for which Sept was grateful.

Landing headfirst in something with the consistency of glue and the odour of rotten eggs was a bit of a problem for the few minutes that it took for Sept to clamber out. Having it stick to him like tar was also not nice (although it did help cover up delicate bits of him that were normally covered in trousers). It got into his eyes and ears and for several minutes he was quite deaf and blind.

When he did eventually get most of the gunk off his face and out of his ears (with a stick), he almost immediately wished he hadn't. The first thing he heard was the howl of several Wargs and they seemed to be coming for him.

Sept froze – partly through fear, partly because he wasn't sure if he had the strength left to run anymore and finally because he was lost and had no idea where he could run to escape these monsters who were entirely built with two purposes in mind: to chase things; and then eat them.

And he probably would have stayed that way were it not for something very strange that now happened. As he blinked away the last of the mud and he looked about, he saw the same cat form he'd seen in the desert, standing not far off under the dark trees. A steady voice, half way between a purr and a growl in his head, said *Run*. In his mind's eye he saw the barn he'd seen earlier. *There!* The voice came again and the feline apparition padded off in the direction of some bushes. Sept got up and followed unsteadily. Almost immediately he came to a rocky track that led from the bog, which had been quite hidden until now. The vision, in his mind's eye, came again of the barn. The baying cries of the Wargs were much closer now, and he probably only had a hundred yards head start. The feline voice came again.

RUN!!

Finally, the boy's frozen muscles sprang back into life. He leapt towards the bushes.

And not a moment too soon. As he sprinted along the path, the howling got louder and more urgent – it was triumphant – they could smell their prey and he knew he'd be within jaw ripping distance very soon. Sept risked a peek behind him and he saw them, beginning to fan out either side of the path, so he could not swerve left or right and escape. Except for the one with an underpant hat, they could see him now and they increased their loping strides to a full run. It was only a matter of a minute or so before they got to him.

Sept was exhausted but, just as his legs were beginning to give out, he finally saw safety ...

❆

The Plogs watched as the door opened and a dreadful, blackened creature, reeking of swamps and rotten eggs staggered in, its breath rasping in its throat and its arms flailing. Gertrude shrank back in terror but the monster seemed not to see her, nor did it see the water trough by the door. Plog watched it fall forward with a splash and was about to run out of the barn, when the door burst open, its hinges splintering. Suddenly the barn was full of hungry Wargs.

The next few minutes went badly for the Plogs.

The lead Warg, with Sept's underpants still wrapped around its huge head, swallowed a goose in one tremendous bite. The rest gobbled up the chickens, Plog's hat and Gertrude's handbag with the pearls. However, even Wargs turn their noses up at someone who washed as little as Plog or were as noisy as Gertrude, so they amused themselves by chasing them around the barn, raking them with their long claws, nipping their fat legs and generally terrifying the life out of the Plogs.

The Wargs only left when the cows started to stampede inside the barn. The Plogs then endured several minutes of being squashed and trampled on by sharp hooves, to add to the claw scratches and teeth marks, while the Hand watched from above, looking as smug as something without a face can do. When the cows did eventually run out of the barn, Plog looked out of bruised blood shot eyes in despair: everything he had planned to steal had either been eaten or run away; his clothes were in rags and his skin had already turned black and blue.

Something made a splashy noise in the water trough.

Remembering the creature who had led the Wargs to the barn, Plog groaned in fear. 'Don't harm me foul beast.'

'Hello Dad,' said a now clean Sept. 'I think that went well. You were right after all.'

Later, Sept was walking home with his battered and bruised parents.

'I really didn't do it on purpose ...' he tried to explain for the hundredth time. How could he have possibly known they had hidden in that shed?

I told you, them being nice wouldn't last. You have to leave, signalled the Hand, now back with Sept, riding on his shoulder. You might have been eaten back there.

Now? signed Sept back.

Yes, the Hand seemed hopeful, bobbing up and down. But Sept looked at Gertrude hobbling along in pain and shook his head.

I can't explain it, but if I go they'll only get worse and who will stop them? he said eventually. *Also, I think they need me ...*

You're kidding, aren't you? signed the Hand. *Remember, you've got a time limit, your birthday is just a few months away.*

... and you won't even tell me why.

And that was the end of the conversation, because the Hand had started shaking again, as if terrified. Sept took It gently from his shoulder and placed It in his inside pocket.

As they continued walking through the dark, the Hand gradually stopped trembling and Sept felt Its comforting warmth through his wet shirt.

Chapter 14

☞ Introducing the Visigoths.

***

AFTER THE WARGS and perhaps because they knew that, sooner or later, the villagers were going to gang up to steal their treasures, Gertrude Plog insisted that Plog hire some bodyguards.

The Visigoths were a terrible, frightening bunch. There were 10 of them, all brothers, and they came from a huge forest that carpeted the tall mountains on the northern shore of the Insidesea many leagues away. And they would chant songs about all the nasty things they liked to do to other people who weren't Visigoths.

Their names were: Herringmouth, Codeye, Rudd-gruel, Spikepuffer, Carpsniff, Doompike, Toadlick, Bonytongue, Daggertooth and Troutsnout, and they all looked exactly alike. So alike, in fact, that it was impossible to tell one from the other, especially when they wore their helmets – the ones with a huge horn in the middle – something they did practically all the time, even when they were in bed fast asleep.

Thanks to them the other villagers became really afraid of the Plogs – Skrewskint had stopped glaring at them when they walked about the muddy main square in their ridiculous new clothes. Even Skrew-skint's two rat-dogs hid behind his bony legs when the

Visigoths marched past in their hob-nailed boots. Sept almost felt sorry for them.

Gertrude watched the Visigoths carefully for a few days, her small eyes calculating. They might have been short – shorter than Sept, even – but they were strong and carried clubs with rusty nails and swords with blades like old saws.

'I wants a Troll Bridge ... thems Visiwotsits are like trollsies, so they can make Mistress Plog a big bridge and charge people money for using our road to go through the village.'

So, two bridges were built, even though there was no river for miles. Each had barbed-wire gates and anyone using the road through Nowhere had to pay a silver coin to pass.

Most people took one look at the strange Visigoths with their long hair sticking out from under their helmets and their sharp teeth and paid quickly.

The only thing the Visigoths did seem to fear was the Hand and, oddly, they treated Sept with a sort of quiet respect. Sept used this to help where he could.

'I'm sorry sir, we really have no money, all I can offer you is this bag of acorn flour and even then we'll go hungry.'

The Visigoth named Codeye stared back at the bald man with his cart full of silent children as if to say, I don't care. His associate Troutsnout sniffed wetly and pointed to the mother's finger.

'B-but that's her wedding ring, it's the only thing of value we've got in the world. You couldn't make her give you that – and it's gold, the sign says silver.' The man looked close to tears, but Troutsnout just pointed again at the small ring and Codeye patted his club.

'That's alright,' said Sept who was passing by on his way home and caught the end of the conversation, 'you can pay us on your way back.'

'Why, thank you, young lad,' gabbled the man and even the small children sitting on the cart looked a bit happier, though still just as damp. Codeye made an odd grunting noise.

'What's that?' asked Sept. 'Are you disagreeing with me?' It was funny, he thought, a few months ago he'd never have dared speak to anyone like that – still less someone armed and as definitely dangerous as Codeye, but a lot had happened to him recently ... and he'd survived. Codeye started to raise the barrier and it was Troutsnout's turn to make objecting snuffling noises with his long nose.

Sept felt heat rise up through his stomach into his hands and the smell of runny mud (and worse) was replaced with a sort of hot dryness. When he spoke again his voice seemed louder and, at the same time, weirdly distant. 'You have something to add, Master Troutsnout?'

Troutsnout let out a squeak of fear and scuttled behind Codeye, who raised the barrier and saluted at the bald man and his family as they shot through the gate.

There, thought Sept, this is why I am staying, but even he knew that wasn't just it.

By now, news of the Plogs had spread and people avoided Nowhere as much as possible. Some of the tradesmen in town had been to see Gertrude, to ask her to take away the tolls. But she refused. So Begre, Flargh, Spew and several others all announced they were leaving.

'Over my deaded body,' snapped Gertrude, then she smiled like a warthog with a nasty plan, 'or yoursies.'

The unhappy villagers took the point and stayed.

Nowhere has got even worse, thought Sept, as he watched them walk away through the drizzle and mud. He didn't even think that was possible.

The Hand, Plog and Sept still went out every day, finding lost coins, trinkets and small treasures, whilst Gertrude stayed at home, out of the rain that seemed to pour continuously from iron skies, and counted the money coming in.

As the days turned to weeks, Sept suspected that the Hand could do much more than simply point at where treasure was; that said, the Plogs were too greedy and probably lacked the imagination needed to think of asking it to do anything else.

In the long dark evenings that Sept and the Hand were left on their own whilst the Plogs went out and spent their money, or stayed in and gloated over it, the Hand would keep Sept company.

Bit by bit, It told Sept about the long life It had lived: first as the Llamara and how It had travelled the hot deserts and lush deltas with Its first master, the warlock.

He was cruel and he kept me chained night and day, unless I was helping him perform his spells. The old meanie.

Why? signed Sept.

He didn't know any other way. In truth, he had no great skill himself, except the binding spell he trapped me with. I suppose he was scared I would turn my power on him.

Did you? The Hand seemed to pause.

Eventually, It said. *I didn't really want to, he was selfish but not exactly evil. Then I realized he would never change. Most wizards are basically just big show-offs. I mean, you only have to look at those hats they wear.*

What happened then?

I wandered amongst the Magee and other magical practitioners of the East. I learned many things, witnessed some of the greatest spells ever seen: parting seas, storms of locusts, armies of the Dead rising … that last one was pretty amazing but I still get the shivers.

But never anything that sounds particularly nice, observed Sept.

You got that right.

So, what happened next? Sept found it fascinating, that he was talking to something that had lived for thousands of years. And the Hand was surprisingly informative.

Then I grew tired of wandering. The palace was my first home. I liked it there … even though …

No-one liked you.

The Hand made a fist in a nodding motion. *Yes, that pretty much sums it up.*

Sept nodded back without saying anything. He knew very well how that felt.

❄

Chapter 15

In which the Hand finds an infernal contraption to satisfy the Plogs. With varied results.

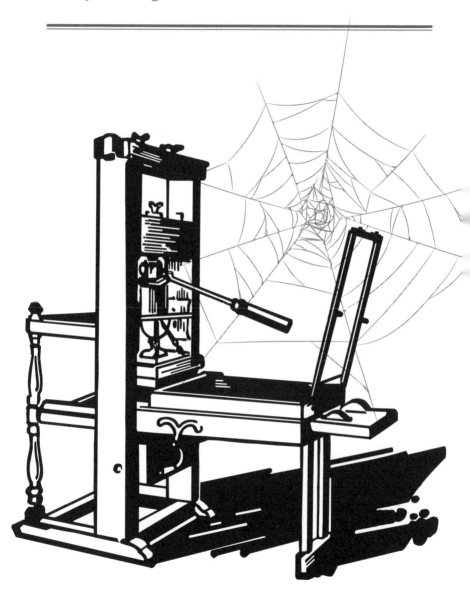

WITH PEOPLE NOW AVOIDING THE VILLAGE, and the Hand having to take them further and further to find treasure, the money coming in began to dry up.

Listening to Gertrude ranting, which was impossible to avoid as Sept's room was right next door to the kitchen, anyone would have thought the world was about to end.

'Soon we'll have nothing left to eatsies!' This was even though they had enough money by now to live comfortably for the next 20 years,

'A diet might do you some good,' muttered Plog under his breath.

'Wossat?!' yelled Gertrude, who had startlingly good hearing when she chose to.

Sept gave up trying to read his book and went to get his boots. Gertrude would expect them to find something amazing – and soon – or there would be hell to pay.

The Hand took the hint and, the very next day, they travelled for miles by cart along many roads that took them to the shore of the Insidesea. It pointed to a

patch of sand. After an hour of digging, their spades hit the top of a wooden crate. Another box. And – like the one in which Sept found the Hand – what was inside would change everything.

It took them nearly half the night to dig it out, with Gertrude shouting unhelpful instructions at Plog and Sept, insisting they keep going. They had to work at night in case they attracted an audience, which only made it harder. Twice they lost the shovel and Sept buried Plog's precious hat at one stage by mistake. If it hadn't been for the ridiculous feathers sticking out of the mountain of sand, they never would have found it again.

It then took them the rest of the night to get the huge crate open with crowbars, jemmys and a mallet.

Inside they discovered a large metal object that looked like a cross between an old-fashioned lawn-mower and a machine for making round things very flat.

Both the Plogs were pretty upset with the Hand at first.

'Scrap iron,' squawked Mistress Plog. 'Is this some sort of jokesey?'

'Gives me the willies,' remarked Plog. 'Looks like it's for torturing people,' he added darkly. They both glared at the Hand who was off making a sandcastle, and ignoring them.

It was Sept who saved the day before things got ugly. 'This looks interesting,' he said, picking up a stack of heavy metal plates at the bottom of the wooden box. He held one up to the lamp they had brought with them.

Ten Pounds

it said in scrolly writing. And

£10

underneath.

He peered more closely, looking puzzled at first, then his eyes lit up.

He went over to Gertrude's large handbag, which was lying at her feet and started rummaging around in it.

' 'Ave you gawn doolali, mad?' Gertrude had been arguing with Plog about who was to blame for them being up all night, far from home with nothing to show for it but a useless lump of machine they had no idea how to use. Now she whipped around like a tiger. 'Feevin' toe rag!'

'No wait,' Sept had a mirror in his hand. It was the one that Gertrude used to put her make up on – she kept it next to the trowel. 'Look at this metal plate in the mirror!' Gertrude Plog folded her arms and looked deeply suspicious.

'Shan't ... Why?'

But Plog, who had the natural curiosity of a career Sneaker, was already staring at it. A big grin spread across his greedy face as Sept held the metal plate up to the mirror.

Ten Pounds

It said, and then

£10

underneath. And although he couldn't read a word, he knew what that sign meant.

They lugged the money printing press (for that was what it was) off the shoreline and loaded it on the cart.

'That's it!' Plog was jubilant when they finally got home. 'No more 'aving to dig up treasure in creepy places, goin' down the pawnshop and hawkin' it there. We're rich, we can print our own money! We just need paper!'

Gertrude Plog looked ecstatic too. 'We can build a new house!'

Sept guessed that some pirates must have buried the machine there but, as the Hand explained later, the story was a bit more complicated than that. In fact, the printing press had belonged to the Governor of the Bank of England but it was old and clunky, and it started to make funny smells when it printed, so he had it replaced with a new one that worked on electricity.

Being very careful, he had it shipped and buried all the way across a couple of continents to the Insidesea, where nobody *he knew* ever went on holiday. And then he went to lunch and forgot all about it.

So, the Plogs set about printing as much money as they wanted and they had an enormous yellow house built right next door to their old house. It was the only thing anyone had built in Nowhere for years and was even bigger than Skrewskint's house. The Plogs became famous in the area and started to attract the attention of rich folk in faraway villages and towns.

This all took several months as hundreds of architects, bricklayers, carpenters and craftsmen and women had to be hired, all because Gertrude Plog wanted to move in before her birthday in August.

Whenever a bill came in for more bricks, or for the new swimming pool that had its own desert island in the middle, or a hot tub, then Plog would sneak off to a room he had built far below ground and print out even more money, which he would stuff into the pockets of his uniform and under his hat.

In Gertrude's head the birthday had become the Most Important Thing in the World:

'It's going to be the most marvelousy party anyone has ever seen!' she exclaimed, all four of her chins wobbling with excitement as yet more delivery men arrived carrying boxes of chocolate buttons, bunting, pink sparkles, balloons and party poppers. 'Everyone will be all jealousy and their eyeballses will explode!'

'Yes dear,' said Plog sounding doubtful.

But not as doubtful as Sept felt.

'This is going to be a terrible party,' he confided to the Hand. He felt a vague sense of dread, as if something awful was about to happen.

It's not too late to sneak off in the middle of the night, his friend replied. Sept shuddered at the thought.

They'd never let me, he signed back. *They'll find me and drag me back, just so I can be around for her stupid party and to see how amazingly happy they are now.*

The Plogs seemed to be getting everything they had ever wished for, but Sept could see that all this magic and money hadn't changed a thing, really. *I don't feel any different, nothing has changed for me.* He still felt just as unhappy as he had before the Hand came along. For, deep down, Sept still had no idea who he was or where he belonged.

And, in spite of all their new money and new clothes, Gertrude still went about in the faded apron she had always worn over her dress. In the front pocket, the menacing outline of the Black Book was ever present. Lurking like some wicked creature.

Being the person who made sure the Plogs did some good with their money became a full-time job for Sept. As far as he was concerned, his parents and Nowhere was all he had – he might as well try to make the best of it. He made sure, whenever he could, that Plog didn't ask too much for the jewels they sold at the jewellers. He even thought up ways to attract the Visigoths' attention, so they spent as little time as possible bullying travellers for money on the toll bridge.

'Spikepuffer's found a rat that died in the sewer last week. He says he's going to gobble it up behind the shed!'

There was a popping noise and Boneytongue and Herringmouth left their post by the toll bridge and ran down the hill at the speed of sound.

But little did Sept know that his helping people was about to come to an end.

'Can't I give her some money?' asked Sept one day, when they were in town. He had been following Plog, lost in his unhappy thoughts, until his attention had been caught by a young girl about his age carrying a small dog. She was selling bags of breadcrumbs to feed the birds although she looked half-starved herself. 'She's not begging and we could have a bird table at home?' In truth they could have had twenty bird tables but Plog just snorted.

'Why pay good money for what the birds can get for free. And if she's so poor, she can work harder. Like us.'

Inside his pocket the Hand scrunched up into a small, balled fist – something It did when It was angry. Sept knew just how It felt.

With a determined look on his face, he thrust his hand deep into Plog's coat pocket and pulled out a bunch of notes.

'Here,' he said to the girl, with what he hoped was a confident smile, 'we'll have twenty bags. Keep the change!'

With a look of rage on his face, Plog stepped forward to grab the money back …

But Sept was ready for him. He stepped between Plog and the young girl who was still staring, open mouthed, at more money than she had ever seen in her life. 'I wouldn't, if I were you,' said Sept, 'not unless you'd like Skrewskint and the rest of them to know how we're getting all this money … and anyway,' he continued, enjoying the look of alarm on Plog's face, which went from bright red to pasty white in milliseconds, 'you made a promise to a certain Somebody to be nice to me.'

As soon as they got home Plog stormed through the door and started to make for the cellar of the new house where they kept the money printing machine hidden from the prying eyes of jealous villagers.

'I'm going to need to print some more money!' he fumed, 'The Cretin keeps giving ours away … all this ink and paper is costing us a fortune,' he grumbled fishing the cellar keys from his pocket, ' – Septimus the bloomin' Saint can get a job and pay for it, if he's so keen on throwin' it about!'

'Whatsies?' Gertrude Plog had been happily separating all the baby pink marshmallows from a pile of assorted colours and eating every second or third one she found. The white and blue ones were going in the bin. 'What's he bin up to?' her eyes narrowed dangerously at Sept who was trying to slip past both of them and up the stairs.

'You heard, ask him – givin' our money away, like it grows on trees!' Sept knew what was coming and he tried to duck, but it was inevitable: Gertrude's arm, like a fat anaconda, shot out and grabbed Sept by his throat.

'Isses this true?' she snarled at Sept.

'Gnarggh ... No!' Sept struggled for breath, his windpipe squashed between Gertrude's fat fingers.

'Liar!' Plog shouted. Sept felt the fingers tighten. He took as much air into his lungs as he was able to.

'It's not *your* money,' he gasped. 'If it wasn't for the Hand and me, you wouldn't have anything ...' The whites of Mistress Plog's eyes began to go bloodshot and her forearm wobbled with the effort as she squeezed more.

'Thinksies that do you?'

Sept's vision began to darken and his knees began to buckle.

BANG!

There was a flash of white light and the air between Gertrude and Sept seemed to expand. Gertrude's whole frame was lifted off the floor and thrown against the wall. Sept felt air rush back into his lungs and his vision returned.

Plog ran forward. 'My wood nymph!' he exclaimed, pulling Gertrude up with a huge effort.

The white light emanating from the Hand continued to shine brightly, throwing out a huge shadow across the vast hallway. The electricity of magic crackled in the air.

Tell them if they don't back off, I'll tear this house down and them in it, signed the Hand.

'It'll destroy everything you have, if you hurt me,' croaked Sept, his throat still burning.

But Gertrude did not seem to notice nor care. She seemed oddly fixed on the Hand.

'Thinksies you got all the answers, you horrible hairy fing?' she hissed. 'But now we've got everthings, we don't need you anymore and I's not scaredy of you anyway.' Her hand fished in her apron pocket and brought out the book she always carried. The cover was so black it blanketed the light from the Hand and oozed out darkness. 'Nasty spidies, with crawly legs get squashed with booksies you know.'

Slowly the Hand's light faded and the shadow weakened. Sept glanced across at his friend and protector and saw It was edging away.

You can stop her, I can't, It signed at Sept.

Real fear, like acid filled Sept's stomach. *I ... I don't know how*.

It was clear that the Hand was terrified of the book and Gertrude continued her advance.

'Yeeesss,' she hissed, 'I sees it now, same reason that stupid old man, Uncles Too-Good-For-Everything, couldn't tells the truth,. Her eyes flicked towards Sept. 'YOU CAN'T TELLS IT TOO!' Her pupils always became small, when she was being cunning and now they all but disappeared. 'The boy's too soft and stoopit to know what's what, but you knows what this is don't you?' She brandished the Black Book and the Hand actually backed away, closer to Sept – as if he could protect It from the advancing Gertrude and the terrifying book that seemed to have so much grim power.

By now the only magic in the room was seeping from its slick cover, like oil from the skin of some long-dead fiend.

Gertrude towered over Sept and the Hand. And she smiled her sweetest smile that was somehow more terrifying than anything that had come before.

'I's in charge now,' she coo'ed in Sept's ear.

❉

Chapter 16

🐾 The Hand finally tells Sept the truth.

Count Ludwig and Countess Ludwiga von Waffleater
(aka The Plogs)
Does graciously invite you to be celebrating the
importantness of the Countess's
Most Happiest
Birthday
On Friday 13th August
Let us know if your coming or not,
ta etc.
7pm on the dot
Carriages if you is rich enuff to 'av 'em

❋

HE'D LEFT IT TOO LATE. Any escape for Sept now was impossible.

The atmosphere in the new house was like being locked inside a submarine at the bottom of the sea: swelteringly hot and extremely dangerous. Sept and the Hand were forbidden to leave and remained upstairs, in Sept's room. Gertrude was far too engrossed in the party preparations to go anywhere. In fact, Plog was the only person who got any relief from the terrible mood that hung over the place like a storm brewing, when he went on his shopping trips into town. Even the armies of servants who came to the house, soon went pale, did whatever they had to do as fast as possible, and then fled.

The Hand, after being threatened with the power contained in the Black Book, was almost meek, like a mouse, and totally under Gertrude's control. All week It had been made to use simple magic to catch the turtle doves that nested in the thatch of the nearby grain towers. It was Sept's job to tie the invites onto their delicate legs.

But Sept was still defiant. Quiet for now, but brooding, his brow permanently furrowed, angry at everything. The pressure in the house was mirrored by the pressure in his head, which felt thick and heavy like his thoughts were made of glue.

Downstairs, Gertrude was screaming at the man who brought the ice.

'It's melty!' she screeched so loud it made the dove in Sept's cupped hand flutter all the more in fright. The invitations on gold card were heavy and the twine to tie them hurt the small birds, who would open and close their beaks in silent fear before flying off painfully, the gold-rimmed invitations weighing them down.

'It's meant to melt, it's ice,' he heard the iceman's voice downstairs, trying to be reasonable.

'Aaargh, stupidest, baldy man, wots broked the ice! Get out, get out of my house and don't funk youz isses getting any money!'

'But that's all the ice I've got, I had to collect it from the mountains, it took me a month to bring it down. I'll be ruined, my family are already eating just dry bread.'

'So what, don'ts care!' Downstairs the large front door was slammed, making the front windows rattle.

'As soon as this party is over, I'm going to ask my parents if I can to go to school.' Sept was trying to tie a noose around the legs of an especially small dove and he didn't look up as he said it.

The Hand remained still. A horrible thought crossed Sept's mind and he looked up from his task.

You'll help me won't you?

The Hand seemed to hesitate. It crouched there, completely still as seconds went by.

Well? signed Sept.

I'm not staying, as soon as this ridiculous party is over, I'm off, It replied eventually and made the sign for the Setting Star. North, which meant only one place. Petunia Rise. Sept wasn't ready for this. He had just assumed the Hand would always stay with him. A hollow, sick feeling like the one he felt when *How to Be Happy* was lost in the storm washed over him, but far, far worse this time.

Sept felt an anger rise in him, it had been brewing in the pit of his stomach for days, perhaps even years, and he had to swallow hard to force it back down.

Well ... you know... so what if you do go ... SO WHAT? I don't care, what's the point of having a magic Hand if it won't help you ... he stopped and looked down.

DESTINY, before you turn 12. leave! the Hand had written on the dirty window pane. Sept stared. He longed to go to school, to have friends, a normal life. Words came to mind, words worthy of Gertrude Plog.

You just want to leave because you're thinking of yourself. All along you've wanted me to go back to my uncle's just so you can be amongst the other magical things in his house! And I don't belong there anymore than I belong here.

No, signalled the Hand with a chopping motion, as in *really* no.

'Yes!' Sept fired right back, suddenly too angry to sign, 'and I wouldn't mind betting you'll leave me as soon as you get there ... ' his voice cracked, ' ... just like everyone else.'

Stop ... feeling ... sorry ... for ... yourself, the Hand signed firmly and very deliberately. The answer hit Sept like a short slap across his cheeks, *you have more going for you than anyone ...* the Hand waved its finger around in a long circular motion, *... anyone around* *here*, It jabbed a finger at him. BUT THE TRUTH FADES. IF YOU DON'T FIND IT OUT FOR YOURSELF SOON, YOU NEVER WILL. THERE ARE NO ANSWERS IN NOWHERE.

Downstairs, Gertrude was shouting again, something about all the mirrors in the house being wrong because they made her look fat.

Oh, Sept, I've wanted to tell you the truth – so many times – but there's a curse that stops me ... it's to do with your uncle and .... and that Black Book. The Hand was now more agitated than ever but Sept didn't really notice. *But if you don't go now, it will be too late ... come back with me ... Sept, you have to listen ...* SEPT? Just then there came a great crash from downstairs as a mirror exploded. Sept's hands clenched instinctively and the dove he held cried out, a single drop of blood beading the end of its beak, like a tear.

The Hand jabbed at him, *Sept ... Sept ...* It jabbed again, much harder. *SEPT!*

Sept snapped!

Years of being second, or third best had been building to this. His whole life being scared, of being laughed at, but most of all it was years of not knowing where he was meant to fit in. It made his head burn with a rage he never knew he could feel.

He was sick of magic and he didn't care about money, neither had ever really been any help to him.

And he didn't need the Hand. He didn't need anybody.

'Why do you keep going on about going back to my uncle's? You never say why? Tell me! If I am your master, you have to do what I say, don't you?' Sept had decided he would find out now.

It's not as simple as that ... the Hand started to reply.

'Yes, it is – tell me, I ... I COMMAND YOU!'

There was a long pause and the whispering of magic came again, this time the voices sounded urgent and worried.

The Hand went very still. With great effort, It made the sign of the Bowing Servant.

So be it.

'Go on!'

Now the Hand began to shake, as if some invisible force was throttling it. Sept suddenly thought about what Gertrude had said about secrets and not being able to tell. He thought about the Black Book and felt cold fear trickle down his back. But it was too late. The Hand, as if in great pain, was signing: It seemed more like a death warrant than a message.

Surviving the storm, Skrewskint's shotgun should have killed you, taming me ... ... You are the same as your uncle and generations in your family before him ... but rare, you are ... a ... WARLOCK ... but you are also special ... so much more than the others I have ever known. You are better than all of them, It signed, the shaking getting worse. The whispering seemed to rise to a roar, the scent of dry sand filled the room and Sept felt like he would choke. *When you were born, your uncle made a terrible mistake. He left a book of magic unattended. A wicked book, of dark spells: the Black Book Gertrude always carries around with her. Gertrude tried to conjure a spell to make her rich and powerful, but it backfired and the whole village was cast down into despair and darkness. Everything good here died at that instant. It affected everyone, including your parents who became mean and twisted, the only way you have ever known them to be ... and you were so small, Sept.*

But even though you were so young, you were the only one who wasn't turned into a terrible person, and you were standing right next to Gertrude when she chanted the words she couldn't understand. You were immune to the wickedness, that is why you are special.

Your uncle's three gifts to you were made out of guilt for letting the Plogs get their grubby paws on the Black Book and in the hope that you would find something at his home that would reverse the spell. He tried to tell you this in his letter when he died, but Gertrude probably made sure you did not see all of it. In spite of everything, you found me, but I don't think I have been much use. I fear I have failed you. It feels right telling you this now, in spite of the curse on anyone who reveals the spell.

Boy stared at Hand.

Your power is a great gift but, like all gifts, it is not fully given until it is freely accepted. Sept, if you do not accept your destiny, your power will pass before your ... the Hand was shaking, *... Sept, you* must *believe me, you need to accept your fate before your twelfth birthday.*

There was a long pause: the longest pause Sept had ever known. The whispering died down to the faintest murmur as if waiting for his answer. His hands unclenched and the dove flew raggedly to earth.

Eventually Sept spoke.

'You expect me to believe that?' he said, his voice like ice. And just like that, the voices fled and the room went back to how it was.

But Sept barely noticed. He had tried everything and failed: he'd tried to be a Sneaker like his dad, a fence like his mum, traveller, hermit, good son, rich kid who helped people. Now, apparently, he had special powers, but, even if he believed it, he didn't care: he just wanted to be carefree, to be normal, to go to school and have friends his own age, not some weird magical, *hairy*, relic.

The words came in a flood of anger. 'It's so obvious, you think I'm stupid, just like my parents! You're trying to stop me, just so you can go back to Petunia Rise where *you* belong – not me!' He glared at the Hand, feeling a new kind of anger, not burning hot, but like frozen steel slicing deep into his kidneys. So,

It was willing to lie to him. He was no more a warlock than any of the other things he had tried so hard to be. At that moment, Sept felt hate that he'd thought only Gertrude capable of. Except, more than anything, he hated himself for being so stupid. For believing.

'There's nothing for me there, there's never been anything for me anywhere, I'm just a weirdo with crap parents and a freak for a friend ... not that it's any sort of friend anyway! I've got ...' he remembered the advice in *How to be Happy*, ' ... I've got choices!'

Sept was too angry to notice that as soon as the Hand had said Its last words, It had shuddered and shrivelled up. Still driven by a rage like wind across an arctic ice sheet, he grabbed the Hand and strode out of his room, down the corridor to the Plogs' quarters. On the mantelpiece sat the strong box Plog used to keep the jewellery they dug up in.

Without any hesitation, he grabbed the Hand roughly and shoved It in.

As he turned the key he distinctly heard a voice in his head cry, '*No! You are not like the others!*' But Sept ignored the voice and concentrated, instead, on his anger. It seemed so much simpler.

That night, Sept dreamt again of the cart, the silhouetted figure with its arms raised chanting a spell, and the weeping.

Chapter 17

☞ Gertrude Plog finally goes proper bananas.

❄

AS SOON AS THE PARTY WAS OVER, Sept was determined to make his parents let him go to school somewhere far away. It would be the last thing he ever asked of them. They didn't really want him around anyway. He would leave them the Hand trapped in Its box. They deserved one another.

After just 3 months, the house was finished. Including a giant fountain.

It was huge – the size of an Olympic swimming pool – and instead of water, Gertrude had insisted on installing a treacle pump. Boiling and churning treacle slopped about like thousands of gallons of gooey lava.

Two days earlier, when they were trying it out, the Visigoth, Daggertooth, had fallen in. Sept thought that his brothers would rush to help him. Not a bit of it. Instead they stood at a safe distance, took out their lunch and settled down to watch. After five minutes, Sept couldn't stand by any longer.

'Um, aren't you going to do something to save him?' he asked.

Herringmouth (or it might have been Ruddgruel or perhaps even Spikepuffer) didn't bother to turn around. 'Nah.'

'But he'll drown in that treacle if you don't.'

'Hur, hur ... yurse.'

Sept looked over at Daggertooth who, to be fair, didn't seem that upset by the fact that the sucking treacle was now up to his middle. He looked over at his brothers. 'Help?' he said without much conviction.

Sept looked at the nine remaining Visigoths.

'Funny,' remarked one.

'Glug,' remarked another.

'Oh, for goodness' sake,' said Sept and he threw Daggertooth a rope.

If the Visigoth was grateful for being saved he didn't show it. In fact everyone seemed quite cross with Sept for spoiling their fun. As far as Sept was concerned, this was just more proof, if any were needed, that most grownups he had ever met were bonkers. That night, Daggertooth slipped off, leaving a note to say he had gone home to sulk.

By now everyone was talking about the new house up on the hill in the creepy village of Nowhere and the strange couple who had built it – all paid for in cash – with new ten pound notes from Old England!

Whilst Plog had been busy ordering the builders around, making sure the architect built everything exactly how Mistress Plog wanted it, Mistress Plog

had been hard at work making a list of all the important and rich people nearby.

She was going to have the biggest birthday party
anyone had ever seen. And after that, everyone would
admire them and want to be their friend. Her dreams
would come true.

By the time her big day arrived, Gertrude was in a
state of extreme agitation. By 7pm she was wailing
that no-one was going to come and her birthday had
been ruined.

No expense had been spared and, as the guests
began to trickle in, fashionably late at 9pm, they stared
in amazement: Plog, dressed in his uniform, which had
been washed and now sported a row of medals, was
flanked by two elephants dressed up in dyed sheep
wool to make them look like woolly mammoths. Each
fake mammoth held a giant bowl of popcorn dyed all
the colours of the rainbow and, as Plog welcomed the
guests by the gates, he invited each of them to try
some.

Plog loved popcorn, especially if it was coloured,
and he could not understand why no-one had had
even so much as a nibble.

In fact, most of the guests, assuming he was some
sort of footman, just ignored him or hung their fur
coats on his head. After half an hour he was com-

pletely covered and no-one could see or hear Plog under a huge pile of expensive clothes.

As the astonished guests walked up the drive, they were then met by the sight of the Plogs' new fountain.

It was windy and the treacle fountain went wrong almost immediately. Pretty soon leaves and twigs got mixed up with the treacle, then the pumps stopped working properly and instead of cascading treacle, it just bubbled, belched and farted like a big, sticky swamp.

The guests had already started to snicker as they reached the main entrance of the house.

Sept, in his best jumper and trousers, was there to greet them: on his own – the Hand was still in the box upstairs. Gertrude had insisted he hold a donkey that Plog had been forced to paint white and stick a plastic horn on.

It was meant to be a Unicorn.

Unfortunately, it just looked like a badly painted donkey with an ice cream cone stuck to its head. When the fountain started to make rude noises, it became nervous and was now braying its head off.

Some of the guests did say hello to Sept but most ignored him, too. He didn't mind. None of them seemed particularly nice anyway – they all walked about with their noses in the air and talked like they weren't allowed to move their lips.

'Ghastly,' he heard one man mutter to his wife.

'Quite,' she replied. 'Is this meant to be some kind of a joke? Surely no-one has taste this bad?' Then she saw the marshmallow sofa. 'Archibald, we're leaving.'

'Already? I wanted at least to have a glass of something.'

'This instant.'

And it got worse – in the guests' eyes at least. They were now all openly laughing or staring in amazement (the wrong sort). In the Plogs' eyes, all this was the very height of refinement – just what they had always dreamed of. If they wanted an avenue of mechanical singing rose buds, one that led up to a large lawn and a solid gold throne upon which Gertrude Plog sat to greet everyone, then why not? Didn't everybody dream of the same thing – if they could afford it?

Later, after champagne milkshakes, they sat down to dinner.

The dining table was made of deep pink crystal and supported at its four corners by pink satin ropes, studded with rubies, that hung from the roof. Instead of sitting at the end of the table, Gertrude had insisted that the stonemasons cut a large round hole in the middle of the priceless table where she could sit on a swivel chair. That way, she could talk to whomsoever she liked and all guests would be able to get the benefit of her amazing wit and surprising opinions as she spun clockwise and counter-clockwise.

Unfortunately, she was too nervous to talk to anyone. She had already seen the looks on most of the guests' faces and she heard the sniggers. There was no sign of Plog and the boy didn't seem to be able to get the donkey to shut up.

The starter didn't do anything to improve Gertrude's mood.

'Oi!' she shouted to one of the Visigoths who were acting as butlers, 'vaht are you do'in youz dumskull, serve me vurst, not those lot!' Gertrude had decided on a foreign accent that day, to make her seem more interesting and exotic.

'Where did you say you were from?' asked an elderly Duchess who was sitting at the end of the table, trying to avoid her tomato ketchup soup sprinkled with hundreds and thousands.

'Er, ahem ...,' Gertrude looked panicky. Suddenly she couldn't remember a single country name. 'Er, Frermany.'

'Grance,' said Plog at exactly the same time. He had finally got out from under all those coats.

The elderly Duchess pushed her plate away with an ill-disguised look of contempt. 'Well, is it France or is it Germany? Surely you must know?'

'Oooh, er.' Gertrude had gone bright red to match the soup … this wasn't going to plan at all. She swivelled back and forth in her chair. Each face she saw was waiting for an answer, people she didn't know … *strangers*, 'neither, it's between the two …' She'd even forgotten how her fake accent went. 'We've got a great big castle don't yew know!'

A real General, sitting opposite her, spluttered. Lucky for Gertrude he'd already finished his soup, otherwise she would have been splattered by the splutter. Lucky for him he'd completely lost his sense of smell and taste when a cannonball hit him on the helmet, which meant he could pretty much eat anything, even the Plogs' starter. 'How can you be between two countries, it's impossible! Unless you're at sea … I should know, I've conquered most of 'em at one time or another … queer bunch this,' he added to nobody in particular.

'Oooh, look, the main course!' said Sept brightly. He never thought he'd think this after everything, but he actually felt sorry for his parents. ' … and doesn't it look …,' but he petered out. There really was no way to describe the main course unless you wanted to use words like *shocking, surprising, alarming* or *very upsetting*.

To be fair, even Plog thought that *Live Octopus Stew* was a bad idea. Quite where Gertrude had got the idea from was anyone's guess at the time – but she'd heard somewhere that all the best restaurants served their fish live.

'What?!' Plog said when she explained. 'You choose your fish when it's alive in those posh places, then they take it back in the kitchen and the chef or someone knocks it on the 'ed with a rolling pin. Everyone knows that!'

Now, the one creature who thought it was a worse idea than Plog was the octopus itself. Four of the Visigoths carried it in on a huge silver platter covered with an enormous silver dome. From under this lid came banging and dull thumping noises, as the octopus waved its arms about angrily in a dark confined space, all on a bed of chopped carrots and white wine sauce.

The moment the lid came off, it launched itself into the air and latched eight strong tentacles around Plog's pudgy face.

'Geddit moff!'

'What?' said the elderly General who was suddenly beginning to enjoy himself. 'Can't hear you man, speak up!'

'Baaargggh, I sned, geddit moff … geddit moff my bace!'

'E-N-U-N-C-I-A-T-E,' someone else said. 'That's the whole problem with the lower classes and foreigners. No elocution.'

Everyone nodded.

Gertrude looked around. Not one of them was helping her husband and she was trapped in the middle of the table. She caught sight of herself in one of the wall high mirrors that ran up and down the length of the dining hall. And Gertrude Plog finally saw herself as others did. In her pink dress, she looked like a great big pudding wedged in the middle of a ridiculous table.

Everyone was laughing. Someone threw a bread roll and guffawed as it bounced off her head, a great braying noise that sounded just like the donkey outside.

Strangers, she thought again. And they had ruined her birthday and her dream of this house and all the money and being able to have everything.

Something in Gertrude snapped.

She reached over and pulled the flailing Octopus off Plog's face with one hand. In a single movement, she hurled it at the General who stopped laughing at once and fell off his chair with muffled cries of indignant alarm. Next, she turned to the lady who'd laughed loudest, taking a handful of her hair and dunking her head in the soggy mess of soup several times.

Then she stood up.

At the force of her standing, the table snapped clean in two. Guests fell off their chairs and into the Visigoths who were carrying food and drink, which tipped in turn onto expensive evening gowns, suits and massive hairdos.

Some people ran for cover, as Mistress Plog started throwing all the food she could lay her hands on at the various guests. 'Youz thinks you can laugh at me do yer? Thinks you'reses somfink special, all ladidah and staring down your great big long noses at Plog an' me, what's invited you to our sumpty mansion with lovely food and you don't have to pay a fing and you fink you can says what you like.' She got hold of the soup tureen with both hands and hurled it at a group of guests, who were immediately drenched in the cold remains of the red ketchup soup. 'Think you look oity toity now? I mebee just some stupid fat lady to yous, but I knows what polite n' nice iz and you ain't politey or even a bit nice. GET OUT, GET OUT, GET OUT OF MY HOUSE!'

Unfortunately, with her last scream she threw her arms wide and knocked over a candle, which caught the tablecloth.

Within seconds the whole dining hall was ablaze. The remaining guests ran out of the large doors at the end of the hall, into the gardens and down the drive, not even waiting for the carriages to pick them up. The elephants stampeded across the perfectly manicured lawns, squashing Codeye and Herringmouth flat on their way, then punched two very large, elephant-shaped holes in the wall and hid themselves in the woods.

Poor old Ruddgruel had the worse time of all. As all the guests pushed past, he fell backwards onto an ornamental cactus by a window. Jumping up, he stubbed his toe on the statue of Gertrude, made of ice, which made him hop around on one leg howling, until he put his other in a large pot of soup that Carpsniffer had dropped when he ran for safety. The pot got stuck on his foot and so he fell over into the fire, which set his hair alight. Hopping from one foot to the other, with thorns still sticking out of his bottom, and his hair on fire, he ran around in circles until Sept threw a bucket of water over him. Unfortunately, Sept had no idea that Ruddgruel was terrified of water, so although his hair was no longer on fire, this seemed to make things worse. Ruddgruel screamed like a girl and ran into the curtains. Knocking himself out on the doorframe, he fell over, and the curtains fell on top of him. Ruddgruel then came to almost immediately, jumped to his hobnailed feet and, forgetting that he had just run into the large pink curtains, panicked. 'I've gone blind!' he wailed and he ran off into the night, with them still on his head.

And that was the last they saw of him.

Sept, still holding the donkey, looked on, horrified.

※

A few minutes later the rest of the house caught fire, even the treacle fountain. The guests all looked like they had reacted in time and would get away safely ... except ...

'The Hand!' Sept suddenly shouted to everyone's apparent bafflement and he turned and ran.

Before the guests started to arrive, he had put the locked casket containing the Hand in a cupboard in his room. He didn't want to look at it – it just reminded him of what was inside and made him feel angry and guilty at the same time. Guilty because when he'd last opened the box, the Hand seemed genuinely ill and Sept couldn't escape the feeling that It was telling the truth about the great risk It had taken by going against the curse. And as for the rest – about him being a great Warlock – he was confused, which just made him angry and he didn't like to think about it.

But now the Hand was in danger and suddenly the only thing that mattered was to save it.

'Can you help me?' he asked a couple who were making for the door. The lady in a huge emerald-studded ballgown just shook her head and the man pushed Sept roughly aside. 'Get out of my way ...'

'But I need ...' he was going to say an adult ... but grownups had never been any use to him and no-one stopped to see what the young boy was so upset about ... and, more to the point, it was obvious that no-one but Sept was going to help save his only real friend.

As he ran down the long corridor from the dining room into the entrance hall, he was shocked to see fire already running up the huge curtains that flanked the stairs and sparks leaping across the chasm of the stairwell and onto the fluffy pink carpets Gertrude had put everywhere. Its thick acrylic material, just like plastic cotton wool, was the perfect base for fires to spread.

And spread it did, the flames rushing through the great hallway as fast as Sept could sprint.

Sept made the stairs at full speed, gasping for breath, just as several small fires broke out along the landing where his room was on the top floor (and where the servants' rooms would normally be in a grand house).

The fumes from the horrible carpet were already starting to choke him, making his lungs heave, and a wave of fire caught the expensive wallpaper. Flames whipping at his heels. Sept felt the hair on the back of his head crackle in the heat as he finally got to the door of his bedroom where the Hand was. He burst inside, staring wildly about the room, half expecting it to be full of black smoke and orange flames. Luckily it was OK for the moment. Feeling a huge sense of relief on seeing the window was open and the room was clear of smoke, Sept wasted no time grabbing the casket containing the Hand from the wardrobe and turned towards the door.

He knew something was wrong when he took hold of the brass door handle and it was searing hot.

In under thirty seconds, the whole of the pink, fluffy and over-furnished corridor upstairs had been transformed into a tunnel of billowing fire, like the inside of some huge dragon's neck. A fish tank, which mercifully Gertrude had not got around to buying fish for, was sending boiling water in frothy cascades onto the floor and it stung Sept's eyeballs just looking at the scene. Feeling sick with fear and lack of oxygen, he held onto the casket even tighter and jumped back into the room, slamming the door.

Sept now ran to the window and looked out wildly. The last guests were already far off down the huge front lawn, running towards the gates at the end of the drive, so none of the adults noticed the lone figure in one of the upstairs windows, nor cared to look back to see if anyone needed saving. There was no sign of his parents either.

Yet again, Sept was on his own and in great danger.

Sept looked down at the flagstones a hundred feet below. Underneath his window was a metal fence running down the steps to the basement. The huge spikes convinced him that jumping was not going to be an option.

Then, the now-familiar whispering started.

No, thought Sept, I don't have time for this, not now.

Sept hissed the voices.

'Go away!' he shouted into the smoky air, 'you're not even real.'

SEPT! The voices were more urgent and Sept felt the Hand in Its casket move.

'Leave me alone!'

OPEN THE DOOR SEPT.

'No!!'

Trust yourself and everything will be fine.

I'm not listening to the voices, Sept thought. 'I'm not listening to you!' he cried. 'If I do open the door it's because it's the only way out!'

He turned back towards the bedroom door, which was now burning through the top panel, searing hot smoke pouring in around the frame. The handle felt quite cool now, almost cold.

He remembered what the Hand had said about King Mithras' wife who had thrown It on the fire all those generations ago and Its being immune to fire. Perhaps the power to not be burned had somehow transferred itself to Sept himself?

Only one way to find out. He stepped into the corridor.

The main part of the house was empty. Apparently, they'd all saved their own skins, and not one, not even his parents, had thought about the fair-haired boy with watchful eyes who had been at the stupid party full of stupid grownups.

This meant that nobody was there to see the small figure, hugging something to his chest, emerge from the firestorm upstairs, touched by the flames but not burned, as he walked calmly down the blazing staircase and into the main hallway. But emerge he did – a few stray glowing embers of ash smouldering on his best jacket, but otherwise quite unharmed and miraculously quite safe.

Ever so carefully, Sept sat on the stone steps away from the house and opened the casket.

If he was shocked when he saw how ill the Hand was, he did his best not to show it, but the Hand noticed anyway. *Stop looking so miserable, I'm not dead yet.*

I'm sorry, Sept signed back, *I'm really, really sorry … I think I know what you did, what you sacrificed …* his hands were shaking. The spell was working its revenge and the Hand was dying. It seemed to be slowly mummifying from the inside out. Sept knew that this was all his fault.

This is all your fault, you know, signalled the Hand. Sept's intake of breath was almost a sob.

What can I do?

You can start by becoming the warlock you are. If that's not too much to ask.

I'll try.

Oh, finally.

... but not for me, for you – so I can make you better ...

Oh, Septimus, the Hand opened Its palm weakly, Its sign for Sept to hold him, *it's too late for me, but not for you.*

But I don't understand, Sept was trying hard to stop the tears. *Look, I can try and fix you ... you should have seen what I did to save you, walking through all that fire, the feeling – it was amazing ...*

No! ... tricks! you can do SO much more ... the Hand seemed dangerously agitated for a moment, then it seemed to sigh ... *No, Sept, sorry, save your magic ... you'll need every ounce of it soon enough. I am dying because everything dies eventually, there is nothing you can do. Anyway, I don't see it as death: I'm transitioning that's all. But you need to accept who you are before you turn twelve, that's all that matters.*

I'm going to find a way to save you, just you see, Sept signed, putting on his most serious face.

Oh, good grief was all the Hand would say.

Chapter 18

☞ Things get out of hand.

'COMES HERES!'

Sept slowly turned away from the Hand.

Even after the fire, the Wargs, shotguns, sand storms and killer wasps, the person who still scared him most in the whole world was standing behind him on the path. Gertrude Plog. Her dirty blond hair covered in ash, her dress torn and fire-blackened.

She had stayed and so had Plog and now she reached out, grabbed Sept with one meaty arm, and pulled him towards the house, back towards the firestorm. Sept stared at her: she looked completely and utterly round the bend. Even Plog was keeping his distance, a nasty bruise over his eye. Despite his fear of this newly terrifying Gertrude, Sept was aware how the house they were approaching creaked and groaned dangerously, like a great beast about to topple

'I was waiting for you, boy. It's all been ruined and it's all your fault ... it's time ... time for the most powerfully book and strongiest spell!' And without asking, Sept knew that she was talking about the Black Book with the bat cover.

'Mum, even the Hand's scared of it – it's dangerous,' Sept felt a rising panic and it wasn't just the fact they were standing in a house that was almost completely on fire.

'Only dangerous for thems that ruins things for lovely Gertrude ...' she screeched, ' ... and they deserves it.' She pointed a fat, trembling finger at where the guests had all run. 'They all laughed at me ... on my birthday an' all ... in my lovely house whats all ruined.' She looked like she was about to cry and Sept almost felt sorry for her again. Then her rage seemed to flood back.

'THATS BOOKS GOT POWER!' she suddenly roared. 'ITS GOT RESPECTIN' AN' MAKIN PEOPLE ALL FRIGHTSEY AN POLITE AN' NOT LARDY DAH AN' LOOKIN DOWN ON YOUS, JUST BECAUSE YOUS A BIT STUPID!' She paused and looked like she was making a visible effort to calm down. 'Well, now's the time to see ...'

Plog saw what he thought was his chance and stepped forward. 'There, there, my dearest, don't be angry on your birthday, I'll get you a big cake – bigger than this one and a fur coat with ...'

'GET AWAY ... DON'T TOUCH ME!' Plog jumped back as if he had been electrocuted by the path. Gertrude Plog took a deep breath. She turned to Sept and began to smile until the smile became a grin. An evil grin that spread across her whole face like an alligator. 'Magic 'elp'd us once afore ... made us strong ... not all nice ... not all weaksies.' She winked at Plog then turned back to Sept. 'You probablys heard the spell went wrong, I say it went right ... so yous and that pet of yours is going to show me those frightsie spells and no-ones going to laugh at uses evir again.'

'No,' was all Sept said in reply. 'You're on your own, now.' The Hand was right all along, he should have left months ago. Why hadn't he?

'She can't read,' whispered Plog, looking pathetic, ' ... *we* can't read. We tried it once before with the Book and got it wrong.'

'Oooh, but youz can!' Gertrude may have looked potty, but her hearing was still spot on. 'Smarty aleccy boy, he can read, oh yes! You show me. You telliz me and I saysiz it!'

Sept turned to Gertrude. He thought of all the years of sleeping in a cold damp bedroom, he thought about only getting leftover potato peelings to eat, being shouted at and getting laughed at. 'No,' he repeated. Sept had had enough of this.

'WHHHAAAAATTT!?'

'I *said* I'm not doing it. It's not your book, it's not even mine and we should go.' There was a loud creak as the house shook, as if in agreement. Gertrude just stared at Sept. He'd never said no to her before like that. He wouldn't dare ... but he was now.

'Uh, oh,' said Plog, sounding a bit muffled, from behind a door.

Sept took a deep breath. 'Anyway, what makes you think some spell is going to solve all your problems?'

At that Gertrude's face changed. It went from mad to spiteful *and* mad. 'Oooh, thinks youz soo clevir, thinks I'm soo stoopid, thinks I don't notice things, can't read, horribliness, fat ...' Sept felt a chill chase up his spine as he followed his mother's narrowed gaze.

Gertrude had spied the casket with the Hand inside. It was still open.

'Gotcha!' she cried triumphantly, grabbing the wriggling Hand in her own pudgy paws as It struggled weakly to get free.

'Leave It alone!' Sept called out. But she just kept grinning.

'Or what? S'pose I slices It with this?' Gertrude picked up a shard of broken glass by the front door and held it against one of the wriggling Hand's slender fingers. Then she opened her mouth filled with gaps and brown teeth. 'What you gonna do about that boysie, if I bites off one of Its wriggly fingies?'

Sept felt his vision tunnel and his head went sort of buzzy. He couldn't fight her. Not his mum. Not if she was like this. His shoulders slumped.

'Alright,' he said. 'I'll help. Just put the Hand down.'

❄

A book-with-no-name, for folk from Nowhere. It kind of made sense, when you thought about it. As ever, Gertrude had kept the Book close to her during the party and now she pulled it from an inner pocket in her huge, ridiculous birthday frock. The pages were as black and scary as he remembered, and Sept felt a shudder of fear alongside a jolt of magic as she handed it over to him.

Sept flicked through the pages as the Hand climbed weakly onto his shoulder ... but ... they were blank! There was no writing. Had this all been some horrible joke? he thought.

'Hurry up, there must be something for revenge in this booksie!' Gertrude gave him a sharp nudge in the ribs.

Sept was thinking as fast as he could, the flames were billowing everywhere and the heat was getting worse by the second.

'Um, I can't ... I can't see anything ....' What would she do, if he couldn't find what they were looking for? It didn't exactly help that he wasn't sure what Gertrude thought she wanted or *needed*. Sept was bright enough to know that magic wouldn't solve every problem, especially when it came to Gertrude Plog. *'There's nothing here ...'.*

'NAAAAGGGHHH! YOU'S STOOPIT AFTER ALL ... TOO GOODS ... ONLY BAD MAGIC'S GOOD

TO ME! The Hand, back on Sept's shoulder, cowered in fear and now Sept began to panic seriously. If she got any angrier, he had no idea what she was capable of doing – not just to the Hand, but to all of them.

In desperation, Sept turned to the last page and, at first, there was nothing there either.

Then Sept felt burning in his fingers – very different from the pleasant tingle of magic – this was a *roaring*, like a stadium of angry voices. He began to get very afraid now as writing seeped through the pages. The letters were dark red, like blood. 'What's that one all about, thens?' The jet black cover seemed to be warm and pulsating, like the skin of an animal, just waking.

'I, er, I don't think it's one for us,' he said instinctively. Right at that very moment, every nerve in his body was telling him that this book was the most dangerous thing he had ever held. Sept just wanted to get as far away from it as possible. At his shoulder, the Hand trembled like a frightened mouse.

'That's it!' cried Gertrude leaning in closer, 'that's it, I **knows** it is. The powerfullest spellsie was hiding in the book, I knews it all those years along.'

'I ... I'm not sure we should be using this ... it ... looks ... dangerous.'

Even Plog looked seriously scared. 'The boy might be right, my dragonfly,' he said.

'Just read it!' barked Gertrude in a voice like sheets of corrugated iron being crumpled.

This is a really, really bad idea, thought Sept. He ran his finger over the top of the page. 'Spell of Terrible Power,' he read out loud.

'Go on.' Gertrude's leered and came closer still.

'By these words, this spell will serve
To give the life that you deserve.
You'll require a looking glass
Say these words and this will pass

... GATHRESTE GAN GARTUAN FESTER KILLE'

'You'll need a mirror,' Sept translated.

But he needn't have bothered.

'GATHRESTE GAN GARTUAN FESTER KILLE, GATHRESTE GAN GARTUAN FESTER KILLE, GATHRESTE GAN GARTUAN FESTER KILLE,' Gertrude was in the hall amongst the flames, racing around half-repeating the words, searching for a mirror. Finding none, she ran out of the hallway further into the burning house. The house was so covered in flames now, Sept wondered if she would return. Part of him almost hoped she wouldn't.

Guests had now slunk back to watch the house in its dying moments, most of them stood on the front lawn at a safe distance. To be fair to Gertrude, Sept saw that some of them were laughing, as if this was Bonfire Night and the Plogs' dream house burning to the ground was the main attraction. The guests were stupid and a bit cruel, thought Sept, but they don't deserve what Gertrude has in mind for them.

Plog and Sept heard her barging through the burning rooms, as the house began to groan as if in pain. And Sept remembered – the oval mirror that hung in the reception room!

'**GATHRESTE GAN GARTUAN FESTER KILLE!!!!!**'

She had found it.

As she said the words, the fiery roof tore off.

The next few moments were a blur. As the Hand ran for the safety of Sept's pocket, Plog and he ducked and tried to find cover under a large marble table that stood by the open door in the hallway. All the time more bits of the house flew off, spiralling upwards in a huge wind that had just sprung out of nowhere.

Sept turned to look up at the sky through the window – it was boiling with black clouds that swirled at the centre, like a forming hurricane, spiralling right over the house.

'Wot's 'appening?' shouted Plog over the noise.

'The spell,' Sept yelled back, '... it must be working ... those words she just said, this must be causing the hurricane!'

Plog looked deep into Sept's eyes, as the front of the house collapsed. 'She's finally gawn mad,' he said half to himself. 'I tried to stop it over the years, but I knew it was goin' to 'appen sooner or later.'

Sept looked up. There was something funny about the storm. The clouds seemed to be taking shape into something horribly familiar. Deep within the swirling depth of the storm a voice boomed out.

'HAR HAR HAR! THIS ISSES POWERFULY-NESS. YOU ARE SO SMALL AND SILLY, I AM GIANTY AND STRONG!' Gertrude's face, immense and yet horribly like her real self now appeared out of the black storm – a gigantic Gertrude Plog-shaped cloud, like a genie released from a lamp.

Sept heard a collective gasp as the former guests looked up at the sky, amusement on their pinched faces turning to fear and alarm.

Before he could do anything to stop It, Sept felt the Hand scrabble off his shoulder. It jumped onto a hall table in front of Sept, turned and pointed right at him, then made the hand signal for *Warlock*.

You can do this, It added.

What on earth are you talking about? signed Sept, but, even so, he felt a faint burning in his fingers and heard the dry whispering.

'WHATS HAPPENING?' Gertrude's storm face peered out of the clouds. Even as an all-powerful genie-storm, her chin wobbled.

But actually nothing did happen.

Diddly.

Squat.

Sept flexed his fingers, but the tingling had stopped. The Hand signed weakly.

Do it now!

'*See! I can't do it!*' shouted Sept above the noise of splintering wood and crashing waves, '... it doesn't work! I'm not a magician, you're the magic one, I'm nobody at all. My parents were right! I'm just rubbish.' The Hand raised Its fingers up in exasperation. It moved forward but then disaster struck: Gertrude gave a great belch, a huge, giant-sized burp, and the Hand was blown across the hall towards Plog by the door. Sept looked up, into his father's eyes and saw what he intended to do. 'No!' he shouted again, just as Plog smirked at Sept.

Then he kicked the Hand as hard as he could.

It flew through the air, Sept reaching out to catch it.

But he was not quite tall enough. The Hand's slender, black fingers brushed his own, like a farewell, as It was blown out into the swirling black clouds that now billowed around the burning house and grounds.

The Hand, his one friend in all the world, was caught in the hurricane Gertrude had called up, and whipped away, high over the house, into the air. It disappeared from sight in seconds.

'Noooooooo!' yelled Sept after it.

Now a finger, the size of a walrus, poked out of the storm. 'COME AND JOIN ME, MY ANGEL, MY PLOG ...'

The instant giant-Gertrude touched him, Plog turned to cloud too.

'NOW WE IS ONE,' she cried, 'WE WILL GO AND WE WILL DESTROY. PEOPLE WILL BE FRIGHTSIE AND NEVER LAUGH AGAIN!'

'Heeeeellllpppppp meeeeeeeeeeee!' screamed the smaller voice of Plog that was soon lost on the wind as his shape was swallowed up in hers.

'BUT FIRST WE WILL SQUASHIES THESE NASTY PEOPLE FOR LAUGHES AT US!'

At that precise moment, images started to rush through Sept's head: of cruel words, getting across the Thorny desert, the desert storm, the box, full of mystery and magic in his uncle's study all that time ago ... something went click.

He saw the view from his recurring dream, of the chanting man with his arms outstretched and the crying. Except this time the cart was clear and so was Gertrude. She was chanting and the people around were crying out for her to stop. He saw the pleasant village he once lived become the sea of mud and misery he had been familiar with all his life.

Then, through the howling wind, the crashing house, the splintering wood and glass flying in all directions, through all the mayhem and sadness, the old man from the cave in the desert appeared before Sept. Despite the shrieking wind, his thin beard and long flowing eyebrows remained still. Slowly, he raised a bony finger and pointed it at Sept's heart. Right at it. Then a second figure appeared, another old man but with more clothes on. Sept remembered the picture on the downstairs table. 'Uncle Xavier?' His uncle nodded and then also pointed a powerful finger at Sept. And suddenly the whole room was crowded with the ghosts of warlocks and wizards past; men in tall hats, magicians from the east with coal black eyes, tall wizards with frowning faces, short ones smiling through twinkly eyes. All pointing. At Sept.

Me? Thought Sept. No!

But the spirits still pointed and nodded.

Me! Thought Sept, again. Why not? For the first time in his life – unfortunately just as it was about to end – he felt a stirring of real hope and a real sense of belonging. Was it that simple? One thing suddenly made sense – he was part of the village, but part of how it was before. If he was a warlock, his name made sense. Septimus – *seven*, the most magical number, he had once read. Finally, Septimus felt something immense and powerful start up from the tips of his toes and spread like warm fire through his body. Something that had always been there but had been deeply buried by his fear and unhappiness.

He listened and the whispering came back.

And finally he could hear what the voices were saying

'*Call the sand, call the sand, call the sand ...*'

A storm cloud fist belonging to Gertrude, slammed into the house and the floor gave away, sending Sept crashing through the floorboards to the cellar below.

'HA!' It went up again like a hammer and Sept, finding himself in the remains of the servants' kitchen, dived for cover. He braced himself to feel Gertrude's huge hand squash him to smithereens ... then he suddenly thought: no.

No. *No. NO!*

He wasn't going to put up with this from the Plogs anymore. He could feel years of pent up anger rising in him, burning through his veins and pounding in his head ...

Not this time. He was fed up with being made to feel small and stupid and being bullied; he was ... Sept raised his hands ...

'COME!' he commanded.

Sept felt pure power rushing from the ground through his feet and body, all concentrated on his hands, which were belting out magic, like magnetic waves. His flexed his fingers and they shot out white hot pulses of light and Sept laughed at how good it suddenly felt; 11 years and 364 days of misery and uncertainty had just burned away. This was who he was, this was what he was meant to be. Sept felt another power, the power of being sure about something. He laughed. He had finally found his place in the world. He knew what he had to do ...

... Sept concentrated and the storm changed course. COME! he spoke the words of command again. Two hundred miles away from the Thorny Desert, a great wall of sand rose up, at least a mile high, far larger even than the storm he had taken refuge from in the cave. Even Gertrude's huge shape seemed small by comparison and Sept noticed that she was looking fuzzy at the edges.

'WHAT'S THIS?' she screamed, 'WHAT'S HAPPENING TO ME? I FEEL FUNNY, NOT POWERFULLY!'

'Oops,' came Plog's voice.

The wall of sand Sept had called up covered the distance in seconds and hit the Plogs, swallowing them up like a giant wave breaking over a swimmer.

'I CAAAAAANNNTTTTT SSTTOOOOOOOP!' she cried

At that moment Sept knew he could destroy his parents. All the pain and sorrow they had caused him ... but something made him pause ...

It didn't feel right, this was not what *his* magic was for: smashing things up, making people do what you want and hurting them if they didn't. That would make him just like all the others. At that moment he could have commanded the sand to blast them to smithereens, he'd never have to see them again, never be shouted at, made to feel stupid, like he had no place. But he wouldn't be that type of warlock

They'd done a stupid thing all those years ago – stealing the Black Book and using it – and everybody in Nowhere had paid for it. But they weren't really evil.

Through the swirling sands, Sept saw himself as a very young boy jumping in puddles and he had looked up at his mother in the house. For once, he could see her face clearly. She wasn't waving back, because she was crying. He felt her regret, before the curse she unleashed by mistake had taken hold, she had known the terrible thing she had done. She had loved him.

If he destroyed his parents he'd be missing the point. Where had the wickedness come from?

THE BOOK!

Sept flexed his mind and saw the Black Book clearly through the storm cloud, swirling; its pages fluttering like a many-winged bat.

Slowly, with a great effort, he turned the sand from the Plogs to pound the Book. The magic in the pages was strong and very old and it fought back, hurling black clouds of counter spells as the sandstorm did its best to break through. Sept concentrated all the harder and felt more power than he could have possibly imagined build up and unleash itself with new fury at the Book's black pages.

In his mind's eye he saw the binding beginning to tear from the spine as it started to shred. The wicked illusion of selfishness and misery woven around the village, and the people in it, unravelled like a funeral shroud being picked apart, one black thread at a time. Until nothing of the Book or its malicious magic remained.

He'd done it! Sept staggered away just as the last of the sandstorm hit him and he passed out.

❄

Chapter 19

The real Plogs. The curse is lifted. Sept finds home.

THE STORM HAD FINISHED what the fire started.

In the misty, damp dawn, when there was almost nothing left but rubble and charred beams, Sept woke and gazed about at the ruins of the house. Everyone was gone. There were no signs of the remaining Visigoths: he guessed they must have run off like the guests.

He had just picked up the dog brush from his uncle's home that had mysteriously survived his travels, the move and the fire, when he saw his father, no longer a storm cloud, climb the cellar steps.

Plog's expression was ashen. 'It's all burned,' he murmured as he walked past Sept. 'The machine for makin' money's all twisted and melted ... useless now ... won't work ...' He looked around. ' ... all gone.' He turned to Sept and actually grinned. 'And good riddance!' exclaimed his father.

And, at that very moment, Sept knew something important had changed. He was still Plog: looked like him, more importantly, smelled like him, but somehow different. For starters, the frown lines around his mouth looked like they turned up now, not down like before, as if he was ready to smile or laugh at any moment, not glare.

'Come on son,' he said.

Walking beside him, Sept stood a little closer than normal – for the first time, in as long as he could remember, it felt safe.

They went off to find Gertrude. Had she changed, like his dad, gone back to what she was before her spell went wrong? They found her sitting on the stone steps that led to the fountain.

'Gertrude?' Plog edged forward as Sept held his breath.

Mistress Plog looked up. Her make-up had melted and black streaks of mascara ran down from her eyes in twin rivers, mingling with the red lipstick that was smeared across one side of her face.

She should have looked ridiculous, instead she made Sept want to help her.

'What is it, my hummingbird?' asked Plog. 'Forget them people. The Hand can find some more jewels n' stuff, an' we'll go shoppin'. Buy you somefing nice, eh?'

'It's not that.' Gertrude's voice seemed changed too, softer now. She cupped something small in her hand, like an injured mouse. She held it out. 'It flew past me, when I was … ' she frowned. 'I can't remembers much … you'll probably laugh, but I was up in the clouds, I think, then I was falling and I reached out … when I woke up I was here and this was in my handsies. It's important I think, but I can't remembers why?' She smiled uncertainly. 'I think it belongs to you, son, but I'm sorry, it's very poorly, it's not moving.'

Sept looked at the Hand and tried his best not to cry.

His mother reached up and stroked his cheek. It felt warm and comforting, but that also made him want to cry too. 'One things I do remembers is it's your birthday. Not much of a birthday, I know, and I'm sorry but we are all threes of us here and you've not been harmed. That's somethings.'

Sept blinked. Get a grip, he said to himself. His birthday, he was twelve. He knelt down, next to his mother, very close to the Hand. 'You said I needed all my magic,' he whispered to his friend, 'that I shouldn't use it all up, but I'm twelve now and, for the first time *ever*, I know exactly what I am. My magic comes from the rocks, the trees, the sky and the water, it comes from life and it can no more be used up than the wind will stop blowing or the sun stop shining because it is the same power that makes everything that is good around us. As long as I don't try and use it for power that's not mine or to hurt people or animals, then there will always be enough for anything I want to do. You're not dead, I can feel that, you're just resting ... we've all had a busy night. But now I want you to feel well again, because you deserve it.'

He took a deep breath.

Stretched out his hand.

And touched the soft down-like fur.

This time the air only felt pleasantly warm and the whispering was like the gentlest of breezes through dry grass, but the light seemed to change all the same: copper-bright as the warmth from his stomach found the tips of his fingers and flowed into the Hand.

'Cor,' said Plog.

The Hand's fingers stirred and the black fur turned to rich gold down, like a rain cloud parting to reveal the sun. It seemed the most beautiful thing Sept had ever seen. His friend stirred.

I am glad it was you, Sept. I have had so many masters over the centuries but none as good and as kind as you. It has been an honour.

'Can you forgive me?

Nothing to forgive, Sept, after all that has tried to harm you, in spite of the wicked spell that corrupted this village, your parents and everything around you, only you remained true to yourself. Only you were untouched and unchanged.

'I'll take that as a yes, then,' said Sept. Then he asked the question he'd wanted to know the answer to most of all. 'Will you stay?'

I could do with a holiday frankly ... but we've got a great future, you and I.

'I think we have,' said Sept.

And, feeling truly happy for the first time in a long time – perhaps ever – Sept turned to see the villagers and some of the guests coming up the hill towards the house. Through the last of the smoke from the still-smouldering embers, Sept saw the sun shining down on the village. Even that looked different: less drab, less dirty, like it had a future.

'We've come to help,' said Skewskint, his craggy face showing concern, not contempt.

At that moment Sept knew his magic had worked: the village was no longer nowhere. It was somewhere. It was home. And this was just the start of things.

The End

Also by **Robin Bennett**

SPACE DRAGONS

**Coming to a solar system near you
in Spring 2019...**

*'A breath-taking adventure through
a vibrantly re-imagined solar system'*

Jennifer Killick,
Author of the **Alex Sparrow** series

Pre-order on Amazon or Waterstones
for prize draw and freebies!

ISBN 9781999884420

W
Waterstones

Watch out on www.monsterbooks.co.uk
for details

CHAPTER 1

The whole universe:
every planet, star, black hole and life form
started with a single atom exploding
into a great void of nothing.
Right after that, came the Dragons.

If Stan Pollux had known he would be spending the rest of his summer holidays in the outer reaches of our solar system, he would have put on different underpants.

The ones he wore the morning when it all began were too tight and had a faded picture of Ben Ten on the back, which made them look like the child super-hero had been specially assigned by the Pants People to guard his butt.

Right now, however, he had more important things on his mind. He looked at the pieces of his broken telescope and thought angrily about his little sister.

'You're so stupid! You broke it and even after you were told not to go in my room, or touch my stuff!' he'd shouted. She was the one who had smashed his telescope but he was the one who got into trouble for

1

making her cry, when it wasn't her fault, according to their mother – although of course it was! She'd knocked the telescope over. It was obviously all her fault.

It was also pretty annoying that Stan hadn't been given any time to sort out the mess until the evening. First it was lunch, then he'd been made to clean up the early fallen apples at the bottom of the garden. Once in a while, he had looked up from what he was doing and saw Poppy peering at him from behind the bushes. He'd scowl and she'd dart off.

Stan knew she was sorry, and what's more he knew she hadn't meant to smash the telescope.

'It's really not nice to be horrible to your little sister all the time, she adores you.' His mother had said. A small, guilty part of him knew that, too. 'You used to play so well together.' And that.

Then they'd been taken food shopping in town, which was almost worse than doing chores and it wasn't until after supper that Stan was allowed to go upstairs and check out the damage properly.

When he got into his room it was ablaze in a blood-red glow from the setting Sun. He got into his pyjamas, watching as the skies had darkened at the top of the window frame and one or two stars winked into view: tiny silver dots millions and millions of miles away.

Stan shivered once more, in spite of the summer evening, closed the curtains quickly and turned on the electric light. It was one of those nights when everything felt weird and a bit spooky.

❄

By the time Stan had got his telescope back on its stand, properly screwed in, and had checked it carefully for dents, the sunset had receded to a fiery fringe on the horizon and the skies were as bottomless and black as infinity itself.

Stan took hold of the eyepiece.

As he was setting it back up, the scope had seemed fine, no dents on the shiny black tube and the stand wasn't bent from where Poppy had knocked it over when she had gone into his room. However, as he moved it, he felt something rattle in the cylinder. He gave the scope a gentle shake and it rattled again, like a loose screw was inside.

Stan's palms were sweaty as he handled the cool tube and it was then that he finally admitted to himself that he felt nervous. But was it just the telescope? Everything felt creepy tonight. He took a deep breath, removed the lens cap and peered down the eyepiece.

Nothing. And, yet, there was something about the deep blackness at first glance that didn't look like right: it almost felt as if he was staring into a hole in Space, and as if, from the end of this long, dark tunnel, something was hiding. And waiting.

Stan shook his head. He was just imagining things. He glanced up ... nope, the Moon was bright in the sky between two large oaks at the end of the garden. Stan checked he was pointing it in the right direction for him to see its reassuring silvery light and looked again.

Nothing. Just a deep, flat blackness. OK, so his telescope was broken! Stan felt his fear driven away by anger. Resisting the urge to rush downstairs yelling, or straight into his sister's room, Stan swung the scope around ...

An evil-looking eye, from the depths of Space, sprang open and stared back.